A QUIET LIFE

BERYL BAINBRIDGE

CARROLL & GRAF PUBLISHERS, INC.
NEW YORK

ALSO BY BERYL BAINBRIDGE

Master Georgie
Every Man for Himself
The Birthday Boys
The Dressmaker
An Awfully Big Adventure
Harriet Said
The Secret Glass
The Bottle Factory Outing
Sweet William
Injury Time
Young Adolf
Another Part of the Wood
Forever England
Winter Garden
A Weekend With Claude
An English Journey
Mum & Mr. Armitage
Watson's Apology
Something Happened Yesterday

Copyright © 1976 by Beryl Bainbridge

First Carroll & Graf edition 1999

Carroll & Graf Publishers, Inc.
19 West 21st Street
New York, NY 10010-6805

Library of Congress Cataloging-in-Publication Data is available.
ISBN: 0-7867-0635-X

Manufactured in the United States of America

◆O◆

ALAN was waiting in the Lyceum cafe for his sister Madge. He hadn't seen her for fifteen years and she was already three-quarters of an hour late. The waitress had asked him twice if he cared to order anything. He said he would just hold on if it was all the same to her.

He felt in the pocket of his black overcoat, to make sure that the envelope containing Mother's engagement ring was still safe. Madge had never liked jewelry. His wife Joan had told him he must ask Madge to foot the bill for having it insured all these months. It was only fair. He'd paid for the flowers and the notice in the newspaper. Madge hadn't even bothered to turn up at the funeral. Instead she had sent that distasteful letter written on thin toilet paper, from some town in France, suggesting that if they were going to put Mother

5

in the same grave as Father it might be a waste of time to carve 'Rest in Peace' on the tombstone.

He was about to order a pot of tea when Madge came into the café, carrying a bunch of flowers. She had an old cloche hat pulled down over her hair. He thought, how changed she is, how old she has become. She's forty and she's wearing a school raincoat.

"This isn't the Lyceum," Madge said. "It's the Wedgwood."

Then he thought, how little she has changed. She handed him the flowers. He found it difficult to catch his breath; in middle age he'd developed high blood pressure, and the walk through the town had tired him.

"What do I want with flowers?" he asked sheepishly, laying them on the empty seat beside him.

"Silly old Alan," Madge said, and immediately he felt disturbed. He hated reviving the past, the small details of time long since spent. Seeing her, he was powerless to push back the memories that came crowding into his mind. It was the way she sat hunched on her chair, elbows on the white tablecloth, looking at him. She didn't rearrange her face the way Joan had managed to do over the years, the way he had. She stared at him. It was this intensity of expression that struck him as child-like, awakening in him that fixation of love he had entirely forgotten. There she sat, after twenty-two years of terrors and triumphs that he knew nothing about, staring at him. When she removed her hat, he had to turn his head. He couldn't bear to see those threads of gray.

"Well," he said. "It's been a long time."

"Yes," she said. She was studying the menu.

"You look well." She didn't have a handbag or gloves. It was obvious she did not see herself as others saw her. He took the envelope out of his pocket and laid it on the table. "It's Mother's engagement ring," he said.

She didn't pick it up.

"I don't want it. I don't like rings."

"It's yours," he said. "You're entitled to it."

"Can I have scones and jam, as well as cakes?" she asked greedily.

He beckoned the waitress and gave their order. He took from his briefcase the list of Mother's effects and told Madge to read it.

"Just say what you want," he said. "Anything you like. The rest Joan and I will take. Anything over we'll send to the sale room and you can have half of whatever it fetches."

"I don't want half," she said. "I don't want anything."

"What was the point of your coming?" he snapped, stung by her attitude.

"I wanted to see you," she said.

The waitress brought the scones. The way Madge ate, he thought she'd come for the food, not him. She got butter all over her chin.

"Listen," he said patiently. "It's only fair you should have what's due to you. There's no money.

She'd only her week's pension when she died. Nothing in the bank."

"Those hats," Madge said. "Those cotton frocks."

"We can't sell the house until the furniture's shifted."

"Who went to the funeral?" she asked.

"Me and Joan and the children. And Mrs. Cartwright from the fish shop sent flowers."

"Nobody else?"

"Read the list," he persisted.

She managed to smear jam on to the edge of the typewritten sheet. She kept on shaking her head. "Don't want the wardrobe . . . don't want the china . . . don't want the sofa . . ."

He began to feel anxious. He'd promised Joan he would sort it out. It had taken him a good six months to track Madge down and arrange for them to meet.

"Just tick what you want," he said. He'd already missed his usual train home.

"I'll have the dancing lady," she decided. "If it will make you happier." She had always been awkward.

She began to talk about his boyhood. How lonely he had been. He hardly recognized himself.

"Rubbish," he told her. "I was never lonely."

"Yes you were."

"Was I?" he said. He hadn't known he was.

She said that was why he played the piano. It was the reason for him being so musical.

"Musical?" he cried. "Whatever gave you that idea?"

"You've always played the piano."

He was astonished. He hadn't played the piano for donkey's years. He doubted if he would know one note from another.

She hinted he'd been spoilt when he was young. Never having to do any washing-up. Avoiding the rows . . .

"Rows?" he said.

"You were never there. You missed all that."

"I daresay," he admitted. "One forgets."

"You never did a hand's turn in the house. You got away with murder."

"What do you mean?" he demanded indignantly.

"Well, you weren't all that upset when Father died. Not really. I cried for days."

"It's twenty-five years ago," he told her helplessly. She had always been a great one for discussing emotions.

She said he had been the favorite. The most loved. Not that she held it against him; she didn't mind.

"Loved?" he said. He thought she was mixing him up with someone else.

She didn't ask him about Joan and the children or what line of business he was in. She seemed to have no curiosity about the present, only the past.

"Who's got the clock?" she asked. "It's not on the list."

"What clock?"

"The one at home. Did you really break it, or was it only Mother picking on you?"

He didn't know what she was talking about. It didn't occur to Madge that home might mean somewhere else for him.

"Which clock?" he said. "I never broke any clock."

And Madge said: "The one in the back room. You weren't supposed to touch it."

Then, prompted by some dimly remembered voice of reproach he heard himself saying with authority: "Don't call it that . . . it's the lounge." It was as though, after they had drunk their tea and finished the cakes, it would be time for them both to return to that place Madge called home.

He had to leave her to go to the station. Madge kissed him on the cheek.

On the train he was annoyed with himself for not insisting she take the engagement ring. He looked out of the carriage window and saw the Territorial Army huts, set on their concrete acre among the dunes. There was a car maneuvering backwards out of a metal gate. He pressed his face to the glass as the train rattled on. They must have taken the huts apart and rebuilt them. In the old days they had stood in the sand, surrounded by barbed wire. . . .

1

HIS mother and father were going to Birkdale to see a solicitor. They didn't say why and he never asked. Mother, in dark gray costume and trembling jacket of silver fox, waited on the pavement for Father to back the car down the path. He needed guidance. The wrought-iron gates had been removed during the war and never replaced; even so he'd managed twice to demolish the brick supports. Mother raised the veil of her gray hat and studied the road for approaching traffic.

"It's all right," she called, shrill and confident. "There's nothing coming."

"Is it all clear, son?" begged Father, not able to trust her, and Alan ran over the grass to the fence and shouted that it was safe. Apart from the 'Lavender' cart, laden with light soil from the outside lavatories of cottages beyond the railway line, the lane was empty.

Madge had departed for the pinewoods immediately after she had eaten her dinner. She had promised not to get her feet wet. Alan had the house to himself until five o'clock, when he must go to Mrs. Evans for his piano lesson. He intended, as soon as his parents had driven away, to prise the bound volumes of the Geographical Magazine from the bookcase and look at the pictures of African women without clothes.

As the car bumped down the curb, Miss Clayton came out of the house opposite and waved to him. A spaniel, sniffing and heaving on the end of its lead, dragged her down the path. He ducked his head in embarrassment.

"Good-afternoon," called Mother, crossing the road and laughing as she went. The dog strained towards her. "No, doggie," she cried, teetering backwards in her shiny black shoes and fluttering her gloved hands in the air.

Father leapt from the car, dapper in his best suit, and raised his homburg hat in greeting. Miss Clayton inclined her head and wound the lead more tightly about her wrist. The dog choked in frustration on the pavement.

"Going anywhere nice?" called Miss Clayton, fingering her headscarf.

"Business," replied Father. "Just business."

He helped Mother into the car. She eased herself into the passenger seat, trailing one pale leg clad in silk. She still laughed. Miss Clayton stood for a moment, smiling and waving, before continuing to the shops. The black horse that dragged the Lavender cart plodded nearer.

"Alan," said Mother, adjusting the folds of her skirt. "Don't forget your music lesson."

"No," he said. "I won't."

The cart, shuddering on wooden wheels, rolled past.

"Ugh," exclaimed Mother, wrinkling her powdered nose at the smell of dung.

He had just time to catch, sweet above the odor of earth closets, the scent of her perfume as she wound up the window.

Father made sure the mirror was at the correct angle; he rubbed at it with a duster. He looked sideways at Mother to see if she was settled. He patted her knee proudly.

"Don't forget to lock up," mouthed Mother through the glass.

She gazed beyond him, at the freshly painted, semi-detached house, set in its winter garden. She smiled fondly.

Alan stood for a while, in the manner of Miss Clayton, nodding and waving at the departing car.

* * *

When he came home in the dark from his music lesson, the hall light shone through the circular window of the front door, lighting the lower branches of the sycamore tree. His father's car blocked the path. If he went over the grass, his mother would be bound to see the tire marks on her flower beds. With difficulty he steered his bicycle along the side of the fence, scraping the han-

13

dlebars across the wood. His father, changed now into his battledress, struggled in the shadows of the brick porch to rewind the hose. He'd been issued with the uniform during the war when he was supposed to be an air raid warden, going from house to house to make sure everyone had drawn their black-out curtains. Mostly when the siren went, he'd hidden under the dining-room table. Madge used to say A.R.P. meant air-raid Pa, not air-raid precautions.

"Mind the blasted fence," Father shouted. He had been washing the car in the dark.

Alan leant his bicycle against the privet hedge in the back garden. He could see the outline of the greenhouse and beyond, the small lighted windows of houses, snuffed out as the poplar trees swayed. He wiped his feet vigorously on the mat in the scullery, so that someone might hear. He always did as he was told and he resented that no one noticed. His mother was sitting in the armchair beside the fire. She had only just lit it and the room was cold.

"Sitting in the dark, then?" he said. His heart sank.

She said: "I haven't got money to burn."

All the same he switched on the light. She sat with her feet on the curb, crouched over the coals. She'd put away her smart gray costume and wore a faded jersey over an old satin underskirt. One of her slippers had tumbled into the hearth. He looked at her broad white foot gripping the curve of the brown tiles.

14

"What's up?" he asked. As soon as he came through the door he felt anxious.

"She's an hour late. After all we told her."

"Well, you should have taken her with you."

He was angry. It was unfair of Madge to put everybody in a bad mood. He was supposed to be meeting Ronnie Baines at the youth club after his tea. How could he enjoy himself if he felt guilty? On the occasions when he left his mother in a distressed state, he never won at ping-pong.

"You try telling her what to do," said his mother. "You have a go, if you think it's so easy."

He went out into the hall to hang his coat over the banisters. He could hear his father muttering on the porch. He had to tread carefully. If he moved too boisterously he would catch the net curtains with his shoulder and tip the vase of cut flowers from the windowsill. The marble statue of Adam and Eve, recently brought down from the landing, was shaky on its pedestal. Even the row of decorative plates, painted with roses and hunting scenes, might roll on their shelf above the door and bounce upon the red carpet. Madge said it was like walking through a mine-field. His mother had a flair for interior decorating; he had heard her remark upon it throughout his childhood. Everything in its place, though never for long. There was a constant rearrangement of rooms, a yearly shifting of ornaments. They had only to grow used to the dancing girl, painted dazzling-white on the dining-room mantelpiece, and she was gone, holding her skirts, now dark green and luminous, above the mahogany bookcase in the lounge. His father said his mother was a menace with a paint-brush: she didn't know when to stop—she would tone in the toothpaste tube to match the walls if she wasn't watched.

"Shut that door," called his mother. "You'd think you were born in a barn."

He would have liked to go to his room then, but it would be too cold and if he wanted to meet Ronnie he must coax Mother into a better frame of mind. Besides, he would have to take off his shoes if he went upstairs. Madge said they might as well be Hindus, creeping around in stockinged feet, getting chilblains in winter, but he could see that you couldn't have nice carpets and tramp all over them in muddy boots. When Madge was older and less rebellious she would see the point. He turned off the hall light and went back into the kitchen, attempting to close the door behind him. The catch was stiff with paint.

"You're making the fire smoke," said Mother.

He shoved harder. He was quite proud of his ability to suppress his feelings when she nagged at him.

"Don't be loutish," she snapped.

The grandfather clock under the stairs chimed in protest. He stood with his back to the fire and wondered how to help her.

"I daresay," he began, "she met someone on the road."

"That's no excuse."

For the last month Madge had been coming in

16

late. She went down to the shore straight after school and thought nothing of arriving home at nine o'clock at night. At the weekends it was even later. His father had taken the car out twice, using up his petrol ration, to look for her. It wasn't right for a girl of her age to be wandering about the pinewoods by herself.

Alan said: "I went to piano lesson."

His mother didn't reply. She sat, slovenly in her old clothes, and stared into the dismal fire. Usually when he came back from music she wanted to know if he'd remembered to sit up straight and arch his wrists. Then she'd tell him to go and shake his coat about in the back garden, to rid it of smells—Mrs. Evans kept pigs in the yard and boiled the swill on the kitchen range; she went in and out, sleeves rolled up to the elbow, to stir the peelings while he played his Rachmaninov prelude.

He heard footsteps on the path outside. Fists beat upon the window.

"It's Madge," he said with relief.

"You fool," said his mother contemptuously.

He stuck his head under the net curtain and stared out into the darkness.

"What blasted idiot turned the hall light off?" shouted Father.

*　　*　　*

They were having their tea, silent under the hanging flypaper, when Madge returned. One moment

17

they were there, the three of them eating their Saturday salad, and then she was through the door, into the light and the fire burning brightly now, her face white under her old school panama and her eyes shining.

"My God," said Father, fork in the air, mouth turning sullen as he saw the dying leaves twined round the crown of her hat. "She'll be the death of me."

She was bursting into tears in front of them.

"Mummy, Mummy, Mummy."

"Sssh," said Mother, rising to comfort her, sinking into Grandfather's chair by the fire. Father said the chair should have been thrown out long ago. What right had the old blighter to hand on his cast-off furniture only fit for the bonfire? Even now, as Mother put her arms round Madge, and Madge threw herself about in a transport of unexplained grief, the arm of the utility chair fell to the floor.

"Damn and blast," cursed Father, struggling free from the table. He tried weakly to hammer the wood back into place with his slipper. "If I had my way," he scolded, "I'd chuck the blasted thing on the Lavender cart. The badge on his A.R.P. beret glittered in the firelight.

"Pull yourself together," Mother said. "Tell us what happened."

"It was awful." Madge kept her face hidden in Mother's bosom. "I was in the woods . . . I didn't want to be late . . . this man ran out of the bushes."

18

"Oh heck," said Mother. She raised dramatic eyes to Father.

Alan thought, I can get out now. They're united by a new disaster.

"It was one of those Germans," Madge said. She had stopped crying. One plump leg, scratched on the calf by brambles, kicked convulsively at the coal bucket. A thin trickle of sand spilled from her ankle sock on to the tufted rug. "He looked like Adolf Hitler."

"Look at the state of you," cried Father in a torment. "Look at that damned thing on your head."

He flung out his arm in passion and set the lampshade rocking. The shadows raced across the wallpaper.

"He had a little moustache," persisted Madge.

"But what did he do?" asked Mother, fearful.

"He chased me."

Madge began to cry again. She looked too big to be crouched there in a lump on the floor, clutching Mother's knees. Look at the effect she was having. Alan couldn't bear to watch Mother's face, small mouth closed tight with suffering, eyes full of dread as she gazed at Father. As if Father knew how to cope. It was cruel of Madge to be carrying on so. Alan knew she wasn't telling the truth—he could tell by her voice. She sounded satisfied, as if she sensed that the danger was over and they couldn't fault her now. Father knew she was lying, but what could he do? He was beaten by her. He turned hopelessly in front of the fire, round and round on the rug like a dog preparing for sleep, hemmed in by the furniture and the dimensions of the small room.

'What happened then?' cried Mother. 'Did he do anything rude?'

"He didn't catch me," wailed Madge.

All at once Father, goaded beyond endurance, bent to snatch the panama from her head. It rose a fraction, and, secured by elastic under the chin, snapped back into place. He stood with a fistful of withered leaves.

"Behave yourself," warned Mother, fierce and protective, straining Madge closer to her heart.

I have to move now, thought Alan, or not at all. If he waited, something unforgivable might be said. Someone would retaliate—Madge would interfere, Father would chuck the sugar bowl at the wall, the three of them would lapse into a silence more brutal than words. He eased himself from the table and took the teapot into the scullery as though to make a fresh brew. He opened the back door and stood by the fence, listening. Behind the net curtains the voices continued; nobody missed him. He left the teapot in its woollen cosy at the side of the drain and wheeled his bike down the path and across the grass. It didn't matter any more about the flower beds. He rode furiously down the street, eyes smarting as the cold air rushed to meet him. He turned left at the telephone box and sped through the gap between the row of cottages ringed by elms, up the dirt bank and into the field. He could see the flare of the sodium lamps arched high above the unseen roundabout at the foot of the hill. He pedalled faster. He would not have cared if his wheel had buckled on a stone and flung him to the damp earth. All that mattered was that he should get away from the house. Try as he might to shut out the voices, he heard them arguing still. ("Wearing my fingers to the bone. . . ." "Don't use that tone to me. . . .")

He shot past the dense mass of the blackberry bushes; the stray briars tore at his sports jacket . . . ("I'm like mud in me own home.") . . . He saw Father, grotesque in his dark blue beret—like a tank-commander stricken by shell shock—clutching that handful of breaking leaves.

He wore himself out; he was forced to stop and rest on the handlebars of his bike. He felt wretched, as if he was hungry, but then he remembered he'd finished his tea before Madge burst in with her daft story and her silly hat. Somewhere behind the wire-netting of Mrs. Allinson's yard, a hen squawked, fighting for space in the coop. He couldn't rid himself of the image of Father, now isolated in the upstairs bedroom, flouncing in worn slippers between the window and the cane chair by the door, while down below in the kitchen Mother and Madge sat whispering, conspiring, eating pieces of jam roll before the fire. How could he possibly enjoy himself at the youth club?

Sullenly he dragged his bike over the ditch and up the slope into the park. He hadn't even washed; maybe his clothes stank of pig swill. If he

21

tried to spruce himself up before he played ping-pong, Ronnie was bound to make some remark about him and Janet Leyland. She wouldn't be there anyway. Even if she was, she'd be too busy talking to her friend Moira to notice him. And if she did notice him, what good would that do? He'd kissed her once, at Donald Eccles's party two years ago, when he was fifteen. In Mrs. Eccles's lounge, in the dark. There hadn't been the occasion to do it again.

All the same, he removed his bicycle clips, so that his trousers would be less creased, before he remounted and pedalled towards Brows Lane. Once on the sloping road, he freewheeled with flapping coat round the corner into the village, past the Post Office and War Memorial, until, leaning sideways so that his mud-guard scraped the curb, he slithered to a halt beside the church. On the cinder path, scuffing red dust, his friends waited. They thumped him on the back; he was popular.

Alan thought of Ronnie as his best pal. He spent a lot of time at his house. Ronnie was neat and slender and slicked his hair back with Bryl-creme. Every day he wore a clean shirt. Alan was paler, more powerfully built. He made the one shirt do for most of the week. He was sent to the barber once a month and his head was so cropped and bristling that he imagined he looked like a convict. Mrs. Baines let Ronnie bring his friends home; even if Mr. Baines was there, she didn't make them stay on the porch.

"Have you got those verses?" Ronnie asked.

"I'm two places off," Alan lied. A prefect at school was passing round a poem, four pages long, about a girl in the women's air force and a sailor. It had been his turn to take it home last Wednesday. He had hidden it in the dancing shoes he used to wear at ballroom classes, and someone—he knew it must be Mother—had removed it.

"I thought you were fetching it Wednesday," Peter said.

Alan didn't reply. He didn't want to think about it.

They swaggered into the church hall and stood self-consciously beside the piano at the foot of the stage. Under the bright lamps, shaded in metal, they were lost for words. Mr. Holroyd and the vicar were sitting at a baize table, making out lists for choir practice. Alan liked the vicar, but when he was with his friends he pretended otherwise. Mrs. Compton was waddling in and out of the kitchen, getting the table ready for refreshments. Cyril, who had married the war widow from the library, was talking to Hilda Fennel. Janet Leyland hadn't come.

"Give us a tune," said Ronnie, opening the lid of the piano.

"I can't," said Alan. It was true; he could only play for Mrs. Evans. The vicar told them to stop messing about. "Table tennis or dramatics," he warned. "You are not here to tinkle the ivories."

"Please sir," said Ronnie coldly, "you've locked up the nets."

It was then that Hilda Fennel called across the hall, loud as anything under the tin roof, "Can I have a word with you Alan?" Hilda was twenty-two and sang in the choir. Last Christmas, during the carol service, she had burst into tears; no one had known where to look.

"What do you want?" Alan said.

Cyril wasn't talking to her. He just stood there, watching her face. After a moment he walked away.

She said: "I don't know how to put it."

He couldn't help her. He stared at his friends opening the lockers under the windows.

Hilda had pointed breasts under a white blouse. He could see them without looking at them. Janet Leyland was more rounded, more of a piece; she kept her arms crossed most of the time.

"It's delicate," said Hilda.

"Oh yes," he muttered.

"It's about your Madge."

"Beg your pardon?" he said stupidly.

He didn't think she knew Madge. Madge never came anywhere near the youth club, nor did she attend the church. The vicar had come once to the house to try to persuade her to join the choir. Mother lit the gas fire in the dining room and there was an awful fuss trying to get Madge to go in and talk to him. Father had to hide in the scullery because he wasn't wearing a collar. Madge talked a lot of tommyrot about worshipping God in the garden.

"Is she sixteen?" asked Hilda.

"No," he said. "Fifteen."

"Is that all?" She seemed shocked.

"She's big for her age," he said lamely.

It seemed to make up Hilda's mind, Madge being a year younger than expected. "I think you ought to know what she's been up to. She was near the Power House this afternoon, with a German prisoner."

"She didn't mention she was there," he said. Madge wasn't allowed near the Power House. It was dangerous.

"They were talking."

"They weren't talking," he told her. "She was running away. She told us."

"She was standing still when I saw her . . . talking."

"Oh," he said.

"I thought you ought to know." She was looking over his shoulder at Cyril.

"Thank you very much, Hilda," he said.

He had played two games of ping-pong when Janet Leyland arrived. Moira wasn't with her. She wore a red frock with a bouncy sort of skirt and thick black shoes. He wanted to play ping-pong again, so as to be occupied, but it wasn't his turn at the table. He was forced to sit idle on the bench beside the kitchen door and watch. In his embarrassment he shouted out things to Ronnie and Peter. They kept telling him to shut up; they hadn't noticed Janet. She chatted to Mrs. Compton. He didn't dare risk turning his head away in case he exposed the livid pimple that was gathering on his neck. It was worse for her, he thought, on her own without Moira. She too, in her way, was exposed. It wasn't that he couldn't talk to her—he knew words to say—it was afterwards that bothered him: asking or not asking if he should walk her home. What if she said yes and they had all that way to go, up Deansgate and past the Grapes Hotel, in silence, bumping against each other in the darkness, apologizing? What would he do with his bike? In her red frock she smoldered by the radiators, doubling her chin as she listened to Mrs. Compton. All at once he heard her say "Goodnight," and she was walking away, brushing against the baize table, her clumsy shoes echoing on the bare boards. He followed; he imagined she would think he was going to the gents. She was in the vestibule reaching for her coat on the peg. She said, "Hello Alan," pushing her arms into the sleeves of a gray worsted coat.

"Oh," he said, slow and casual. "I didn't see you. Have you been here long?" His ears burnt and his heart beat fast.

"I'm just off," she said.

"Been keeping well?"

"So-so," she admitted. They met during the week and twice on Sundays, for Morning Service and again at Evensong. They faced each other in the choir stalls; he had never sought her out before. As she did up the buttons of her coat, she confided: "I saw your Dad on the train the other day. He's very merry."

He said: "Yes, he is that."

"He's always so jolly. He called me a bonny girl."

She sounded pleased. Father called Madge bonny and she was on the fat side. He supposed Janet was too, but it was more evenly distributed.

"Your mother wears lovely hats," Janet said.

She seemed obsessed by his parents. She was ready to go, insulated against the January night, her gloves on and her collar turned up about her neck.

"Shall I walk you home," he said. "It's time I was off."

"Better not. Mother wouldn't like it."

Still, she dithered in the chilly vestibule, patting her dry curled hair, waiting.

"Maybe tomorrow," he said. "After Evensong . . . We could go for a walk."

"Maybe," she conceded. And she went, pink and self-righteous, out of the door.

He was relieved, in a way, that Mother wouldn't like it. He had already found that it was usually better to look forward to something than to experience it. But he couldn't settle to ping-pong any more. He told Ronnie he was leaving early because he had Latin homework to do. It wasn't true. He hadn't given Mother notice that he wanted to use the dining room. He did his studying in overcoat and scarf—minus his shoes—resting his books on an old blanket kept for the ironing, so that he wouldn't harm the table. He wasn't allowed to use the upstairs room; there was nowhere to work except the bed and she forbade that in case ink spilt on the eiderdown.

*   *   *

It was Mother who had retreated upstairs, not Father. He was sitting in the dark with Madge, listening to a play on the wireless. With both armchairs pulled close to the fire, it was difficult to enter the kitchen.

"Let me in," pleaded Alan, trapped between the door and the chair-back.

"Shut up," said Madge. "We're listening."

He had to stay where he was, one leg in the scullery, until she was ready to shift. The wireless was balanced behind the curtains. It was too big for the windowsill and jutted out into the room; the valves never burnt out, but it had cracked across the front in three places and been patched together with strips of black adhesive. Because of its size Father was forced to sit at an acute angle at the table, eating his food hunched over his plate. Mother wanted it thrown out. Once she nearly succeeded. She was upstairs shaking the bathroom mat out of the window. It was damp and heavy and slipped from her fingers on to the aerial stretched from the kitchen window to the top of the fence post. Father was sitting listening to the news at the time. The wireless leapt on the sill and toppled between chair and table. A man inspired, Father flung himself forward and caught it in his arms. He swore like a trooper.

"It's over now," Father said, standing up and switching on the light. "Let the lad in."

His beret lay on the floor beside the coal bucket. He had one piece of black hair that he combed the wrong way to cover his bald spot; without his hat it hung down over his ear. He bent to poke the fire, cautiously resting his hand on the mantelshelf above. Mostly he misjudged the distance and straightened up too soon, striking his head in the process. He had a small scab, dark brown and never quite healed, to show for it. He sat back in Grandfather's despised chair, wiping his hands on his battledress. He looked mournfully at Madge.

"It was grand," she said. "When his little girl went missing . . ."

Father nodded. They were both overcome. They stared, harrowed, into the flames.

"You look as if you've had a good laugh," Alan said, struggling to sit at the table.

Father gave him a sheepish look and blew his nose. He was moved to tears by a good play. He was often found mooning in the firelight, handkerchief at the ready, listening to the Third Programme. It afforded him some sort of outlet.

Alan eased his collar and winced.

Quick as a flash Father noticed. "Oh yes," he said. "Have we got another boil?" He jumped to his feet to examine and probe.

"Get off, Joe," shouted Alan, jerking his head away. It was the name he called his father when he was apprehensive or angry. Father thought the

29

world of Stalin; he said the Russians had won the war.

"Keep still," bade Father. "Let's have a look." He prodded the inflamed skin with hard thumbs.

"It's only a pimple," protested Alan.

"It's a boil. You'll need a poultice."

He told Madge to fetch the kaolin. Alan had to take his chair into the hall so that she could get into the pantry. He called to her to bring out the tea caddy while she was about it.

"You can't make tea," shouted Father. "Your mam's hidden the tea pot out of spite."

He ground the kaolin mixture into a paste with water. He laid out the scissors and the roll of lint. Alan took off his tie and removed his collar stud. Madge fingered the swelling on his neck.

"Don't do that," said Father, pushing her hand away. "You'll make it spread."

Father was fond of playing the doctor. He tore a portion of old sheet into a square and lined it with lint. He shaped it carefully, as if he was making a nest for a fledgling. He encouraged himself as he worked. "That's it . . . There we go . . ." Spooning the kaolin on to the pad, he knelt on the hearthrug, lock of hair dangling, to warm the mixture at the fire.

"Not too hot," warned Alan.

"Go to sleep," said Father.

When he was ready he told Madge to push Alan's head down.

"Not yet," cried Alan. He half turned; he wanted to see what it looked like, the thing that was going to hurt him.

Father advanced with the pad held in one upturned hand, like a waiter balancing a tray. He scowled.

"Bend over. The blasted thing's burning a hole in me palm." He slapped the poultice down.

"Is it hurting?" asked Madge, squatting on the floor and peering up at him.

"It's perfectly all right," said Father, as if he was in a position to judge.

Alan refused to cry out. His eyes smarted with the pain. The paste seared his skin and squelched upwards from the cotton pad into his hair.

"Good lad," praised Father. He wound another strip of sheeting about Alan's throat, making a muffler for him, not too tight, not too loose. "I'm off," he said, when it was done. "I'll lay a towel on the pillow for you." And he stomped upstairs to bed, full of good humor.

"You could have said thank you," said Madge, folding the remains of the lint and picking threads of cotton from the rug.

Alan couldn't answer; he wasn't yet in control. He tried to rest his head on the table, but the bandage constrained him. He pushed his chair backwards to the edge of the hearth to give himself more room. Madge couldn't pass him to go to the scullery without falling into the fire.

"I'll never have children," she grumbled, crawling under his legs on hands and knees. "Nailed up in little boxes, no room to stand up."

"You were seen this afternoon." He felt vindictive. "Near the Power House."

"It's like cruelty to animals," she said. "I don't

know why they ever bothered . . . they're as miserable as sin." She was in the scullery, rinsing the cup and spoon under the tap. "It's worse than burning in hell fire." Once she started she could be very extreme.

"Put the guard in front of the fire," shouted Father from the upstairs landing.

Madge came back into the kitchen and started to drag the armchairs to the wall. Alan turned stiffly to watch her. She had a broad forehead, a prominent nose and pale lips. When she was younger it seemed to him that she resembled a bird, eager and watchful, running about the house, pecking at him; she was easily startled. After that she grew cheeky and moved more clumsily. At fifteen he thought she was at her worst: her full cheeks gave her a spiteful look.

"You were seen," he repeated. "By Hilda Fennel."

"Hilda who?"

"The girl in the choir. She saw you with that German."

"So what?"

"You weren't being chased," he said. "Not when she saw you. You were chatting to him."

She didn't seem bothered. She pulled a strand of cotton through the gap in her front teeth.

"Don't do that," he said irritably.

"I've been sucking grass," she said. "There's a bit stuck."

"What were you saying to him?"

"I wasn't," she said. "I told you. I was running."

He didn't know how to handle her. She had an answer for everything. She stared him out with round deceitful eyes.

After a while she said: "You want to work out why that Hilda whatsit told on me."

"Don't talk daft," he said. "She was worried. She was quite within her rights."

She grew indignant then. "Worried?" she said. "I bet she was. She was necking with that man."

"What man?" he asked, startled.

"The man who married the war widow from the library."

"Rubbish," he cried. "She wasn't."

"And I wasn't chatting," she said. "I was running."

He'd tried in the past to reason with her, but it was never successful. He blamed his parents for indulging her, letting her play the clown. All through her life she'd got away with things. Like the time the man came to the door when Mother was out, asking if there were any old clothes to sell and Madge gave away her fur gloves and his new school blazer. She'd have parted with his raincoat too if Mother hadn't come home. And the time before, years ago, when she was caught showing her bottom to the evacuees over the railway line. He would have been hit with the strap for less. They scolded her all right, but they weren't disgusted, not deep down.

"Poor old boy," Madge said, touching the sheeting bound about his throat. "Who's a pimply old Alan?"

She left him to put up the fireguard and lock the back door. When he crawled into bed he found it difficult to lie comfortably. He mustn't mess the sheets with the poultice. The rough towelling spread on the pillow irritated his ear. He daren't fidget too much in case he woke Father. Unlike Madge, he hated disturbing anybody. He could hear her coughing in the next room. She coughed every night, as soon as she lay down, for ten minutes or more. A harsh bark, like a dog. They took her to the doctor every three months or so, but he couldn't explain or alleviate the condition. It happened as frequently in summer as in winter, so it wasn't the coldness of the rooms at night.

He heard his mother moaning through the wall. She said peevishly: "Please Madge, I'm worn out."

Madge was unobliging. She rustled the sheets. The bed springs jangled. She went on whooping in the dark.

·2·

HE HADN'T known that his grandparents and his aunt were coming to tea. It meant he was expected to stay home and play cards. He ate breakfast while Father made the fires and scrubbed the scullery floor. The worn string mat was bundled behind the privet hedge. Being Sunday it wasn't seemly to hang it over the fence in full view of the neighbors. Madge sat on the table to be out of the way of the tidying; she wasn't asked to assist because she was always more of a hindrance than anything else. Mother lay upstairs in bed, her breakfast on a tray.

"It's not right," moaned Father, running in and out of the back door with mop and pail. "It's not man's work."

At morning service, Janet Leyland pretended he was invisible. She stood in the oak stall holding her hymnbook, a white frill at her throat, looking right through him as she sang the responses. He was sick of half-smiling and nodding his head in her direction. In the vestry he told Ronnie loudly that he wouldn't be coming to Evensong. He couldn't tell if she heard or not; she was into her coat and out through the door before he had his jacket off the peg.

Mr. and Mrs. Drummond came on the three-o'clock train. Aunt Nora arrived later, by bus. They were always invited together. Alan supposed it was to be rid of several obligations at one sitting.

Father shut himself in the scullery and Mother watched the road from the bedroom window. When she saw her parents turning the corner, she called downstairs: "They're here. Tell your father, Alan."

Father, when told, said: "I'll bet they are," and stayed where he was.

Mr. Drummond was tall and bulky; his leather shoes were blood-red with polish. He strode into the house, unbuttoning his grey topcoat. Mrs. Drummond, weighed down by her brown fur coat, scurried into the hall.

"Hello Alan," she exclaimed in surprise, as if he was the last person she expected to see. "Look who's here," she told her husband. "If it isn't our Alan."

Grandpa tipped his hat like a conjuror and flopped his gloves inside.

"I know, Mother," he said curtly, bundling her into the lounge.

He warmed himself at the fire, gazing out at

the bleak garden, while Alan helped Nana out of her fur.

"That's a good boy," she said, sinking down into the gray armchair and making herself comfortable. She was so short her black court shoes dangled above the patterned carpet.

Grandpa took her coat into the hall to lay over the banisters. He wandered into the front room and nosed about in the piano stool. He had been an accompanist to some singer when he was young; Mother boasted about it.

Alan was left with his grandmother beside the fire. She rustled in a brown dress, the veil of her hat hooked back over the brim so that she could see out. She had a bulge in her rouged cheek where she kept her peppermint candy.

After a while they heard Mother coming down. Nana twisted in her chair—"Is that you, Connie?"—but Mother had gone into the front room to talk to Mr. Drummond. He could hear them greeting each other as if she was a little girl who had fallen down and grazed her knee. "Oh, Dad, . . ." "There, there, Connie."

He tried again to persuade Father to go into the lounge. He tugged at the scullery door and caught him making a beetroot sandwich.

"What are you doing, Joe?" he asked, exasperated. "Mr. Drummond's here."

"What's that to me," cried Father, defiant in his best suit.

"Don't talk soft," snapped Alan. "You can't stay here."

Father bridled. He pranced a few steps up and

down the scullery to show how little he cared.

What right had he, thought Alan, to fume and bluster, to fill the house with anxiety? What was the point of the fire in the lounge, and the sardine sandwiches and the cakes set out on the tea trolley? How ridiculous the man looked, flaring his nostrils and curling his lip in that fashion. Madge said it was on account of his puritanical upbringing: he'd never been encouraged to study himself in the mirror; he had no conception of how exaggerated were his gestures or his facial expressions.

"You can't stay here," he repeated.

"Go to blazes," said Father.

All the same, he wavered. He wiped his mouth on the roller towel behind the door and after a moment went sulkily into the lounge. Gray and peaky, he stood at the hearth and attempted to be civil.

"So you're here again," he said.

"It's a grand fire," said Mrs. Drummond, used to his ways.

The room was painted white. On the desk was a photograph of Madge, dressed in a party frock of gauze, a ribbon in her hair. There was a low table by the fire, with a glass vase filled with early daffodils. The curtains moved in the draught. Beyond the french windows the black pagoda, bare of roses, rocked on the brown lawn.

Alan had to be careful of the starched antimacassar behind his head. There hadn't been time to bathe the poultice from his neck; he wore a check muffler held in place with a safety pin.

He wondered if Janet Leyland would be disappointed that he couldn't walk her home. He went upstairs to look out of the bedroom window. The road was empty of her. He knew she would never come this way—she lived on the other side of the village. Still he strained his eyes to catch a glimpse of her red frock walking towards the house. There was his Aunt Nora, head bent against the wind, hurrying up the path.

He didn't hear Mother come into the bedroom, until she shouted at him. Startled, he turned to face her. Under her pencilled eyebrows she stared at him without pity. He might have been a stranger.

"What are you doing in here? How dare you, you great lout."

He was astonished by her outburst. What harm was he doing? He hadn't sat on the pouffe covered in yellow taffeta, or dented the counterpane of her bed, or twitched the curtains a fraction out of place as he stood at the window.

"Shut up," he said, stung by the unfairness of it.

Aunt Nora knocked at the front door. Mother in her best black, sequins on the bodice, trembled in front of the looking-glass. She opened the drawers, lifted the lid of the powder bowl on the dressing table.

"Get out," she said. "Don't you ever let me catch you in here again."

He often thought that she was punishing him for something he had done when he was small. She had left Father for good, three times—packed a bag and gone to stay with her parents. She'd come into his room and asked him if he wanted to go with her. She never asked Madge; she held his sister's hand as if she would never let go. He longed to be with his mother. If only she had *told* him to leave, not asked him to choose. How could he abandon Father? And each time she closed the front door, he thought he would never see her or Madge again. He thought they had left for ever. When Mother came back, the relief he felt made him stubborn; he could never run to her.

His grandparents, at the arrival of Nora, acted thunderstruck.

"Good Lord, Nora," Grandpa said. "Fancy seeing you."

"Is that Nora?" cried Nana. "Well, bless my soul."

"I turn up everywhere," said Aunt Nora drily. She looked like Father, with her thin mouth and her overemphatic eyes. She had a mocking laugh, low and infectious, that ended in a loose cough and a spit into her handkerchief.

"Call your mother," ordered Father. "Tell her your Auntie's come."

He wouldn't. Let Madge do it; he was sick of playing games.

Madge dominated the room. She pirouetted in front of the fireplace in her Sunday frock, telling them about school. She glanced at herself in the mirror as she spoke, as if to make sure she was there. "I'm top in English . . . Miss Williams is a dope . . . Don't you think they ought to abolish Geography?"

Mother came down and peered through the door.

"Oh, you've arrived, Nora," she observed huffily, as though his Aunt had been hiding from her.

Aunt Nora rolled her eyes sardonically. Her shoulders shook with silent laughter.

"How's business, Dick?" asked Grandpa.

"Can't complain, Mr. D.," said Father, for once.

Alan wasn't sure what his father did for a living. His interests were varied. He didn't have an office or go to work at regular hours. He conducted his business on the telephone in the front room, or in public houses in the city. He wasn't a drinker. Sometimes he took Mother with him, dressed to kill. Only last week he had pulled off some deal involving a factory in South Wales. He came off the telephone rubbing his hands and smiling delightedly. He and Mother whispered together in the scullery. She chuckled with satisfaction. He scribbled down figures on the back of an old brown envelope and added them up. The house seemed brighter, more spacious. Mother said it was time Alan was fitted for a new suit. He didn't want one; he hated the idea of spending the next twelve months worrying about his creases, and being reminded of how much the material had cost. Years ago Father had been more prosperous—that's why Mother married him. Then a slump came and he lost his money and with it the big house and the maid and the rose garden. Even so, he owned a car, and no one else in the street sent their children to private schools. It was because he was an honest man and a good manager. It was a sin to buy things you couldn't afford. He'd been in shipping, he said. Since then he'd been in paint and cloth and timber. Laid out on the boxroom floor was a quantity of corks in cotton bags with drawstrings. Alan understood he had just finished being in medicine bottles. Madge said he was a commercial traveller, but it wasn't that simple. He didn't go from door to door with a little suitcase full of boot polish.

Father helped Mother wheel in the tea trolley. He handed round napkins and patterned plates. The firelight and the sandwiches made him cordial. He began to discuss an acquaintance who had accumulated a fortune in scrap metal. He was impressive about percentages and profit margins.

Grandpa listened politely. "Get away," he remarked at intervals. "You don't say."

Mother talked to Aunt Nora about hats. She loosed a remnant of material from under the clock and held it to the light.

"Would you say that was green or blue?"

"More blue than green," said Aunt Nora, wrinkling her eyes with effort.

"Nonsense," said Mother. "It's green."

She ignored Mrs. Drummond. Madge said she disliked her because she was common and wouldn't improve herself. It was true that when Grandpa went on his cruises before the war Nana had stayed at home. She didn't care for his butterfly collection either, or the Everyman Library books he bought every month. Nana's idea of a good read was "Home Chat" or "Red Letter." Mother had never forgiven her for confiding to Madge that she'd worked in a lollypop factory as a child. She told Madge that Nana was making it up out of mischief, but Madge knew better. Grandmother had also had rickets when she was a baby. Madge told all her friends at school. It would have killed Mother, had she known. Whenever she took Nana out for tea in Southport, she bullied her and spoke waspishly. She criticized her clothes and her posture. When they got up to leave, Madge said Nana pocketed the tip Mother left under the muffin dish for the waitress.

The afternoon wore on; the day darkened. They cut into the sponge cake and drank several cups of weak sweet tea. Madge begged to be allowed out to the shore. Grandpa dozed before the fire.

It was time to play cards. Alan fetched the Indian table with the brass tray, from under the stairs. The closet was damp and smelt of mildewed clothes. He leant his face against the old raincoats and thought of Janet Leyland at Evensong.

They had to lift back the settee to set up the table. Grandpa pushed at the rug with his shoes to maneuver his chair out of the way. Mother never said a word.

"Can't I go for a walk?" whined Madge. "I don't like cards."

"No you can't," said Mother. "We've visitors."

Father went upstairs to find his cotton bag full of pennies. He tipped them on to the table and they spun and rolled across the brass tray that was honey-pale in the firelight. He enjoyed the thought of winning a few pence off his father-in-law. He gave them back when the game was over. He enjoyed that even more; he thought Mr. Drummond was a mean old skinflint and it gave him pleasure to show him up. It made Alan unhappy, watching Mother, beady-eyed on the settee, praying that Grandfather would refuse, and being disillusioned time without number.

They played Rummy for Madge's sake; she was hopeless at anything else. She lacked concentration and was inclined to cheat. Aunt Nora played a losing game. She bit her yellow arm in anguish when she was left with a palmful of aces. She lay back in her chair and covered her mouth with her handkerchief.

"That time in Blackpool," she wheezed. "When we had a Pontoon night."

Nana nodded. Shrewdly she counted her cards.

"It was the air, Nora. It was that bracing."

Grandpa sat with his watch chain dipping across his belly. He kept them all waiting while he studied the hand he'd been dealt.

"It's been beautiful," said Mother. "The last few days."

"Have you been anywhere nice?" asked Nana. "Been for a run in the car, have you?"

44

"Cold but not windy," said Mother. "Until today."

"In Spain," recalled Grandpa, "it was mild this time of year. The sun on the mountains . . . the white houses in the villages . . ."

"Beautiful," murmured Mother, gazing at him with love.

"There was nothing to disturb the eye, no blot on the peaceful landscape. You could hear the bells. While in the distance the—"

"What's wrong with the lad's neck?" asked Aunt Nora.

"Boils," said Father.

Madge grew restless. She slumped against Mother and let everybody see her cards. She wanted Grandpa to play the piano.

He said he would, all in good time.

"I love us singing round the piano," she said. "We all seem close." They thought she was an old-fashioned child. Alan knew what she meant.

When Grandpa played, they stood shoulder to shoulder.

"Bless this house O Lord we pray
Keep them safe by night and day
Bless the people here within
Keep them safe and free from sin . . ."

sang Father, with his arm about Mother.

"Let's go into the front room," nagged Madge. "Let's play the piano."

"The dining room," corrected Mother.

All the same, she wouldn't allow it. She

couldn't have two rooms messed up in one day.

The game continued. While the scores were added, Alan went into the hall. He was still smarting from his mother's attack. He opened the door a moment to cool his face. The branches of the sycamore tree tapped the pane of the upstairs room. For years Father had been threatening to cut it down—he said the roots were undermining the foundations. Every spring Mother in her gardening gloves tugged out the new shoots growing in the borders, choking her antirrhinums and her dahlias, and every autumn Father gathered the rust-colored leaves that choked his drains. He burnt them in a heap beyond the greenhouse, beneath the tall intact poplars. They would never cut down the tree. It was part of the house. Mother complained it blotted out the sunshine, but if it didn't she would surely draw the curtains to keep the carpet from fading. Madge called it a willow. She said fancifully that she liked a garden with a weeping willow tree.

Mother said it was time to make another pot of tea. "Or perhaps," she suggested, looking at Mr. Drummond, "you'd prefer something stronger?"

"That would be welcome," said Nana.

Aunt Nora dug her in the ribs with anticipation. Father was putting his cards down and counting his pennies.

Grandpa said: "Did you make that appointment, Connie?"

Mother went pale. She laid her fingers fanwise over her breast.

"What appointment?" asked Father, low and menacing.

"The solicitor chappie I advised her to get in touch with," said Grandpa. He wasn't looking at Father's face.

Father hurled his pennies across the room. The women cowered backwards on the settee.

"By God, I might have known," he cried, bent double over the brass tray as if he had been stabbed.

"That's it," said Madge, jumping to her feet. "I can't stand any more." And she ran out of the room.

Alan caught hold of her in the hall. She was trying to open the front door.

"Don't," he warned. "Don't add to it."

There was a confusion of voices coming from the back room, rising and explaining and threatening. They could hear Mother crying out, wild and scornful—"Take no notice, Dad. Don't demean yourself." Then Father, desperate with jealousy, stuttering in anger—"No n-notice. N-no notice. God damn it, the mean old bugger."

Madge fled up the stairs.

Aunt Nora came into the hall to fetch her coat from the pile humped over the banisters.

"Don't go," said Alan.

"I'm not stopping here," she said. "It's a mad-house." She struggled into her sensible coat. "Do you know," she hissed, "how much it cost me to come here to witness this little carry-on?" She looked old and crumpled, itemizing her expenses,

47

jabbing her finger against his chest: "There was the bus fare and the chocolates for your Mam. There was me ciggies on the journey. There was knitting wool for your Madge."

"I know," he said. "Don't go."

She jammed her felt hat on her head and opened the front door. He followed. She walked rapidly along the deserted Sunday road. It was cold and he shivered as he trailed her. Anything to get away from the house. A flash of electric blue came from the railway crossing as the Southport train sparked on the frozen rails.

She took pity on him. She stopped and fumbled in her bag.

"Go home," she said, handing him half-a-crown. "You'll catch your death."

"Will you be all right?" he asked.

"Don't talk silly. I'll be on the bus in no time."

He didn't like her going home through the night, on her own, back to her little empty house, without a fire, without cakes in the pantry, without a family.

"I reckon," she told him, beginning that throaty cackle, "that it is them you ought to worry about." And she strode off, starting to cough as she reached the crossing.

He waited till the bus arrived. She turned to wave at him. The lighted windows slid past: a man and wife, a boy alone, his Aunt Nora spitting into her handkerchief.

He saw his grandparents coming out of the house. He crossed the road and hid in the shadows of the elm trees. First Grandpa, then Nana walking three paces behind, clutching her bag like a squirrel.

Father had stormed upstairs to bed. Mother tidied the lounge, gathered up the pennies from behind the cushions. She picked the tipped vase up from the rug and hurled the blooming daffodils into the fire. White and mute she fetched a rag and rubbed at the carpet; she looked as if her blood had drained away with the flower water. Alan wheeled the trolley into the scullery. She followed him.

She said: "He can't control himself."

"No," he agreed. He felt disloyal, bitter, and yet she needed him.

"My poor father," she said. "He was only trying to help."

He couldn't share her sentiments but he kept silent. He nodded hypocritically.

"He thought it would be a good idea. It's in all our interests."

"What shall I do with the leftovers?" he asked.

"You see, he thought the solicitor might sort things out."

"Shall I put them on the fire in the back room?"

"The lounge," she said.

"Or in the bin?"

"Listen to me," she cried, holding his arm and badgering him. "We had to see that fellow. You don't know what it's been like all these years. Not knowing if anyone would check up. Why should Nora benefit?"

"Did you say thank you for the chocolates?" he said.

"And he's not getting any younger. Anything might happen. What if—"

"I don't want to know," he said, thrusting her hand away. "It's none of my business." And he went into the front room and chucked the crusts of bread on to the fire, on top of the singeing daffodils.

·3·

HE WAS coming home from school with Ronnie. At this hour the carriage was half-empty. They lolled about and put their feet up on the seats. Through the windows the flat coastline was blurred with rain. Alan was a day boy at Derby Hall, six miles away on the outskirts of the city, and Ronnie went to the grammar school in the same suburb. Now they were in the sixth form they didn't have to wear their caps, nor were they forced to exercise in the yard at break. They went bareheaded in the street and after their dinner they sat loafing in common-rooms. These twin privileges were a sign of their maturity. For the rest, they were told what to do and when to do it.

"Do you realize," Ronnie said, "if the war had lasted a few years longer, we'd be treated as men." His brother Michael, at the same age, had marched through Europe.

"I daresay," said Alan.

He didn't really care—he had ceased to notice that he was regimented and ordered about from morning till night. He'd begun to fall behind in class and his teachers warned him he might do badly in the exams. It hardly bothered him. He had been good at Latin and History and considered fair at science. But lately, neither lessons, nor games on the windswept playing fields, nor the other distractions offered by the school, held his attention. He wasn't unhappy or disturbed; he merely sat motionless at his desk, a placid expression on his face, thinking of other things. Only at moments, when some foolish prank was played, did he start up in his seat and like a child at kindergarten join in the sniggering of his friends. Most of the time he thought about Janet Leyland—the way she looked at him, what she said, a certain mannerism she had, of touching the lobe of her ear when she was unsure. He wasn't lovesick or anything like that. He wasn't off his food. It was more that he was engrossed in her acceptance of him— his ideas, his cleverness. She thought he knew a lot. He came from a household that regarded men as inferior; they were fed first and deferred to in matters of business, but they weren't respected. Janet even liked his hair-cut. It was a revelation. It made him think about the future, the complexities of earning a living and acquiring possessions. Several years back, he wanted to be a farmer—he was good at milking cows and stooking corn, he drove the tractor for Mr. Ledbetter in the holidays.

Mother, however, had decided he should study municipal law and become a Town Clerk. He tried to envisage himself returning home from work to Janet Leyland, sitting in a similar kitchen, fully furnished, with the proper quota of cutlery and china in the cupboards. He imagined he would be sentimental and talkative; he'd tell her about politics and history and she'd listen, nodding, holding his hand, her slightly popping eyes looking into his. She'd wear a nightie, he assumed, when she went to sleep. His mother wore her slip and cardigan in bed, and Father retired in his combinations; Alan had never seen either of them without clothes. He supposed they would come to tea on Sundays. He knew, somewhere at the back of his mind, that he could only hope to be an extension of his parents —he'd step a few paces further on, but not far. His progression was limited, as theirs had been. He'd read Mendel's theory in the fourth form—color of eyes or structure of mind, it was all the same. It needn't mean he'd end up with nothing to talk about, only that there'd be some things over which he had no control, certain preferences and priorities. He'd always be polite and watch his manners. Most likely he'd vote Conservative, in rebellion against his Father. He would want the house to be decorated nicely. If possible, there'd be a willow tree in the garden.

"What did Lacey say when you told him you'd lost that thing about the sailor?" asked Ronnie.

"I didn't listen," he said.

The train was passing the rifle range and the

row of nissen huts that housed the German prisoners of war. There were red curtains hung at the windows. The barbed wire fence rolled in disrepair across the wet sand.

Ronnie said: "The vicar's invited the blighters to Morning Service. He must be batty."

"Our Madge was chased by one the other night. So she said—she came home bellowing, anyroad."

"Get off." Ronnie was scornful. "Your Madge isn't frightened of anything."

He thought Ronnie was right. Madge only cried when she was caught out in a downright lie, or when it suited her to be dramatic. He knew that some of the local girls had been seen fraternizing with the Germans, down by the shore. It was worse than going with Yanks. He wouldn't put it past Madge to be hanging about the camp, though God knows what she hoped to attract, wearing her mac and her knee socks. When she was twelve she'd brought home a young soldier from Harrington barracks. Mother and Father were out. She said she was only following Father's example, being kind to our gallant lads in khaki. She was referring to Dunkirk and the time Father had fetched three members of the forces from the reception centre in the village and put them on deck chairs in the garden. "It's not the same," Alan told her, worried that the neighbors had watched from the windows. She made eggs on toast for tea. There wasn't any harm in Madge—she was only a child —but he hadn't forgotten how the soldier ate his poached egg with his fingers. Alan had been forced to put down his knife and fork and shut his eyes; it turned his stomach. "Pardon," the young soldier had said. "Is he saying Grace?"

"What does your Mum think?" asked Ronnie. "Has she complained to the Commandant?"

"Not yet," said Alan. "She's very bothered. They both are."

Since his grandparents' visit, his mother and father were not on speaking terms. It was back to Madge carrying messages between the two of them. "Mum says can I have the money for the Insurance man? . . . Dad says has Roly Davies rung yet from South Wales. . . . There's a funny noise coming from the pipes in the loft. Will you have a listen? . . ." Father came home at his usual time and sat upstairs in the cold. There wasn't anywhere else for him to go. Maybe he called at Aunt Nora's and she gave him food—he didn't eat anything Mother prepared. When she went upstairs directly after tea, he came down. He rushed past her violently in the hall, making the clock chime, averting his face as if her breath smelled. He listened morosely to the mutilated wireless. Mother read her library book at the bedroom window. When Alan wheeled his bicycle down the path he knew she was there, behind the branches of the sycamore tree, watching him. His legs felt like lead as he rode away. Madge came in from school, changed out of her uniform and marched whistling along the dark road to the shore. No one else he knew behaved like she did or had such freedom of action. At her age, the sisters of his friends were in the Girl Guides or going to tap-dancing classes. Somebody ought to speak to her, for her own good. The difficulty was to sustain his sense of responsibility throughout her prevarications. He didn't want a lot of irritating chat about religion being in the pinewoods and the back garden, and didn't he feel near the Holy Ghost when he played the piano? The way she talked you'd think God was living in their greenhouse. She drove him mad with her airs and her silly romancing.

"They shouldn't let a stupid kid like her out on her own," said Ronnie. "She's a blinking menace. She always was."

"They don't," he protested. "They keep a tight rein on her."

Madge was barely fifteen and she did as she pleased. Nothing stopped her, neither Mother's suffering nor Father's bullying. She went carefree as a bird, in her school raincoat and her old panama—as if it was high noon in an Indian summer—toward the railway crossing. The night was black as pitch down there on the shore, the wind blowing in from the Irish sea, the waves booming as they broke upon the beach. There were still undetected mines and unexploded shells in the woods. The enemy planes had unloaded their bombs before reaching the sea. She could be blown to bits as she stumbled between the dense and groaning pines. She came home drenched with rain, her hair tacky with salt; in the morning, at the back step, he could see the heap of sand she had emptied from her shoes.

"Don't you remember," said Ronnie. "That time in Hall Road?"

"Hall Road?"

"When she went into that bombed house and walked along the rafters."

"No," said Alan.

"Your Dad gave you a hiding."

"Don't talk daft," he said. And he swung his satchel on to his shoulders and stood by the doors, waiting for them to open.

They had a mug of tea in the porter's room, under the arch of the station. Above their heads, along the slopes of the bridge, in six feet of earth the crocus bulbs waited to germinate. The ticket man liked young boys; he was forever mussing Ronnie's hair and telling him he had a skin like a girl. For all that, they felt like men, sitting at the solid table, swearing, drinking their strong black tea.

"You nipped off bloody quick after choir practice," said Ronnie.

"Shut up," he said, imagining he was smirking all over his face. He'd walked Janet home twice now and kissed her once, on the mouth, behind the laurel hedge in her front garden. He dreamed he saw her in the bath—he couldn't wait for summer to come and for her to be rid of that heavy coat and those woolly jumpers.

The room was a warm cave; the great fire glowed in the iron stove. The air was heavy with the smell of engine grease and coal dust. Outside in the small village, life was ordered and predictable. There were no noises in the night since the siren had ceased its sudden swoon of alarm—only the shuddering of the Lavender cart as it rolled past the silent houses. On the coastal road the woods had shrunk to a small wedge of pines; the trees were no longer a jungle, laced with the webs of poisonous spiders—the time had gone when he could climb to the top of the sand dunes and think he was El Cid reaching the sea. Nothing happened that he couldn't understand. Here, with the trains rumbling behind the granite wall and the lantern swinging above the unswept floor, he could for a brief moment imagine that anything was possible.

"Are you coming to camp this year?" asked Ronnie.

"I might," he said. He hadn't been allowed to go last time because the year before he'd arrived home with impetigo. His mother had to buy him long trousers so that the neighbors wouldn't see the scabs on his legs.

"It was wizard, that week we had in Windermere," Ronnie said. "That dope Wilson falling in the lake—"

"It wasn't Wilson. It was the little brat from the wool shop."

"It was smashing climbing that mountain. We were miles up."

"It was a hill, not a mountain."

"It felt like a mountain," said Ronnie. He fiddled with the heap of tickets stacked on the table. He smiled widely. "Wasn't it smashing, though?"

"Smashing," agreed Alan. He'd hated it. He

couldn't stand the damp nights and the insects crawling over his skin.

*   *   *

Mother was in Southport and Madge was on her own, drawing at the kitchen table. Without a fire the room was shabby. The paint was peeling from the pantry door. Mother didn't bother much about the kitchen—she only decorated the rooms they scarcely used. Madge said she'd had the day off school.

"Are you ill, then?"

"My cough." The tip of her tongue protruded. She was crayoning a reptile with flames coming out of its mouth.

Alan grunted. He thought her cough was something she cultivated. It didn't stop her walking in the rain.

"That and the checks," she said, laying down her pencil. "He wanted me to sign another one this morning."

Alan flared up at that. "Why do you cause trouble? Why can't you do as you're told?"

He dumped his football boots on to her pencil box to aggravate her.

She took no notice. Behind her head the flowered paper was scraped clean, exposing the plaster. When Madge was younger she used to lie face downwards on the polished surface of the table and spin round and round, scuffing the wall with her shoes. It was sheer vandalism. Then as now, she could do with a thundering good hiding.

"If he'd explain what it's all for," said Madge. "I wouldn't mind. You can't be too careful about that sort of thing. He's a fool. My name's not just a squiggle on one of his checks, you know. I'm at a very sensitive age. He can't wipe me off, like fingerprints on a jam jar."

It was no use arguing with her. He didn't know himself why it was necessary for her to sign Father's checks. She had to write her name on documents as well. Father folded the papers so she couldn't read the print, leaving only the dotted line at the end of the page. You could hear them battling away upstairs at least once a week—Father thumping the dressing table where he'd laid his bit of paper and Madge crying out: "Why should I? I want to know why?" She complained to Alan that Father was spending her money. "Don't be stupid," he told her. "You haven't got any money." She said it was obvious she had; otherwise why did the bank need her signature? "Someone may have left me a fortune," she argued. "A dead relative or something." They hadn't got any dead relatives apart from Father's parents, who had died poor as church mice, when he was a boy. "Anyway," she persisted, "I talk to all kinds of old people. I always have. I'm very interesting to talk to. How do you know one of them hasn't left me war bonds?" For some reason Mother sided with her over the check signing. She said repeatedly that Father ought to make better arrangements.

Alan went into the hall to take off his coat but changed his mind. It was too cold. He didn't dare put the gas poker to the fire before Mother came back.

"What time's Mum coming in?" he asked Madge.

She shrugged. She was drawing a border round her picture.

"Well, you won't be going out this evening at any rate," he told her with satisfaction. "Not after staying off school."

"Yes I will," she said. "A bit of air will do me good."

He had to clench his hands to keep control of himself. "Listen," he began mildly. "You shouldn't go out in the dark."

"It was for a new suit for you," she said, suddenly remembering. "Shall I sign the blinking check?"

"I don't want a new suit," he shouted. "Will you concentrate on what I'm saying. What do you get up to every night . . . in the dark? You can't see the beauties of nature."

"Shut up," she said.

"Well, what do you do?"

"Nothing," she said.

"Traipsing about the shore—"

"I don't traipse," she said.

"There's unexploded bombs," he told her.

"Rubbish."

"It's dangerous on the beach," he shouted. "You should stay in the house."

"In the house?" She looked at him contemptuously. "Don't you think it's dangerous here?" And she stared dramatically about the kitchen as if there were bogey men peering out from the leaves of the rose-patterned wallpaper. "There's worse things than bombs, you know."

He flung his scarf on to the table, enraged. He wished she wouldn't talk like that. It made him want to hammer sense into her with his bare fists.

After a moment she said: "I don't go on the beach, anyway. Not right on it."

"You're running wild," he muttered. "It's not normal." He regretted instantly his choice of words. He thought she would launch into some drivel about normality being relative. For once she kept silent. Encouraged, he said: "Don't you see what friction you cause in the house? They're worried sick over you."

"It's not me, Alan," she said. "It'd be all the same if I stayed in. It's money . . . and that solicitor."

She didn't seem to grasp that it was the trouble she caused him personally that was his main concern. He was long past marshalling the reasons for his parents' behavior—it would be like emptying a cupful of ants into a butterfly nest for safekeeping. All he wanted was for Madge to stay indoors at night, so he needn't return to find his father jumping up and down, demented, at the curb.

He ought to switch the wireless on before Father came home, in case he was in a worse mood; they turned it on for the sake of the neighbors, to deaden the unbridled language and the slamming of doors. But he couldn't talk to Madge properly against a background of dance bands. He stood indecisively behind her chair, looking at the wireless, trying to make up his mind.

"Do you like it?" she asked, holding up her drawing.

"Will you concentrate on what I'm saying?" he demanded, tapping her on the shoulder.

She sulked. She sat offended at the table, scraping her pencil box up and down the wood.

"You'll make a mark," he warned. "Stop it."

She pouted; if she'd had a penknife handy she would have engraved her initials out of cussedness.

He remembered the time she wanted to come with him to Ronnie Baines and he wouldn't let her. She hid behind the bins and when he came out of the back door, she thumped him over the head with the yard brush. He sank to his knees. Mother gave her a clout over the ear but she broke into a fit of coughing and it ended up with Madge being put to bed and waited on, while he had a lump on his skull as big as a fruit drop.

"Try to be reasonable," he said. "I'm concerned for your welfare, that's all."

She looked sideways at him, and then down at the drawing.

"It's smashing," he said patiently. "You're good at Art."

She smiled a little.

Cautiously he asked if she went anywhere near the camp.

She didn't know where he meant.

"The P.O.W. camp," he told her.

"What are you getting at?" she cried indignantly.

"Well," he said. "You were seen with one of those chaps."

"By a couple of adulterers," she shouted, jumping up from the table in fury. "I know what you're insinuating"—he noticed there was a blue crayon mark, like a vein, on her temple—"Just because you're a dirty bugger yourself, writing verses about sailors, you think everybody's the same."

He had to retreat into the scullery to avoid hitting her. The cheek of it—ferreting about in his cupboard. "Where have you hidden it?" he demanded. "You tell me where you've put it or I'll knock your block off."

"I'm sorry," she said, upset at what she had done. "I threw it down the lav. I thought I heard Mum coming upstairs and there was nowhere to hide it."

He switched on the wireless and flung himself into the armchair. He couldn't look at her.

She made him a cup of tea, though God knows what Mother would say if she came in and caught them.

He didn't say thank you. He drank it without a word.

She sighed several times to show how sorry she was. At last, too late, she wanted to tell him where she went every night in the dark. She never coincided with anyone if she could help it. When he was happy, she felt sad, when he closed up like a clam, it was then she wanted to be open and confiding.

"I don't want to know," he told her. "I wash my hands of it. Do as you please."

She didn't persist. She laid the cloth for the evening meal, tidied her pencils away, peeled potatoes at the sink. She had the nerve to ask him if he had any money. He hadn't and he told her so. She went upstairs to the front bedroom; he could hear her moving about above his head.

Mother came in, dressed in furs, face delicately pink from the walk along the promenade at Southport. She didn't comment on the unwashed cups and saucers left on the draining board. She inquired if he'd had a nice day at school and if Madge had taken her cough mixture. Her tone was perfectly pleasant but he was aware at moments that she eyed him coldly; he was puzzled, knowing that it was Madge, not her, who'd found the poem in his dancing shoes. A letter had come from his housemaster by the morning post, giving the date of the parents' coffee evening. He would have to be fitted for a new suit, no doubt about it.

"What's wrong with my uniform?" he asked.

It was out of the question—it was to be quite an informal affair, just the sixth form and the parents, and they'd all be in lounge suits.

"You as well," he said, but she didn't hear.

"Is your father home?" she wanted to know.

"Not yet."

"I expect he's gone creeping round to that

sister of his," she said, eyes glittering with malice behind the little grey veil of her hat.

Alan found it absurd that his father couldn't admit he saw Aunt Nora daily. When he himself married, and he supposed he must—how else would he be taken care of?—he intended, if she hadn't been blown to pieces before then, to visit Madge as often as he pleased.

* * *

Later that evening, Mr. Harrison called at the house with a friend. Mother and Father were caught in the same place, trapped together in the kitchen—Mother had popped downstairs to fetch her spectacles. When the knock came at the door, Madge was out into the hall and letting the callers in before anybody could stop her. She led them straight into the kitchen. It was unheard of, people dropping in without an appointment, Father in his battle dress and Mother barelegged, her skirt torn at the hem. They stood white-faced and shaken, united by the calamity.

"Come in, come in," said Father, recovering first, darting glances at Mother. He had a funny smile on his face, welcoming and yet fanatical.

The small room was immediately crowded. Alan was edged into the scullery.

"What an imposition," said Mr. Harrison. "I do apologize, but I assure you it was expedient."

His friend, a tall man with insets of velvet on

the collar of his long black overcoat, stood pressed to the wall.

"Don't mention it," said Father, dragging the armchairs away from the fire, desperate to make space. It was no use ushering the visitors into the lounge; without a fire laid several hours in advance they ran the risk of frost-bite. In such a dilemma, and dressed as she was in her indoor clothes, Mother sacrificed Madge.

"Bed, darling," she said. "Come along."

She lowered her head as if shy. By an effort of will she kept her hands from her face, to hide the smudged eyebrows and mouth devoid of lipstick.

"I'm off out," cried Madge, outraged.

"Silly little sausage," Mother said, pushing her firmly into the hall.

Madge could be heard protesting as she was propelled by force up the stairs. She started to cough directly overhead.

Mr. Harrison was a scholar and had known Father for six years. According to Father they'd met on the train and struck up a conversation over some article about Stalin in the morning paper. Mr. Harrison had been lucid on the history of the Russian people. He said Rasputin wasn't the devil the books made him out to be. Mr Harrison had visited the house on a few occasions, mainly out of doors in the summer time. He spoke at length about the decadence of pre-revolutionary France and about his sister Nancy who was failing fast. Mother yawned and yawned in the golden sunshine. Only once had he been invited to proper tea

67

in the front room. He addressed Mother as "she who is beyond praise," and slopped his bowl of tinned pears on the cloth. Mostly Father met him on the train. He said it was obvious, by accent and turn of phrase, that the man was educated. Why else would he be so careless in his dress and carry on so many volumes of books under his arm? It was an edition of the poems of Swift that had brought him to the house that evening. He needed it, he said.

"I shall fetch it," reassured Father. "Say no more."

Alan couldn't remember Father ever reading poetry. He listened to it on the wireless but he didn't look in books. Mother was the artistic one in the family—she'd taught Madge to recite "Come hither Evan Cameron, come stand beside my knee . . ." that and "The Slave's Dream." Father had once sketched a tulip for Madge, but it was hopeless and she threw it in the fire.

Mr. Harrison introduced his friend as Captain Sydney. He'd had a dreadful experience with Rommel. Father, lock of hair dangling, greeted him effusively. He himself hadn't been fit enough to fight—he had done his best in the A.R.P. Mother came down, changed into slacks, her nose freshly powdered. She had a turban wound about her hair. Captain Sydney said he couldn't sit down.

"Why ever not?" said Mother, twinkling roguishly at him. She bustled in and out of the pantry carrying a packet of cream crackers and a pot of jam.

"I have," he said, "a gathering . . ."

"Oh dear," said Mother, and she gave a little scream of hysteria as she took a piece of wrapped cheese into the scullery.

Mr. Harrison's sister was still failing, but no more than usual. "Tragic," mourned Father, shaking his head dismally.

Mr. Harrison stared into the fire. He wore a spotted bowtie and evening-dress trousers and held his thin tapering hands in an attitude of prayer.

"And the teaching?" inquired Father.

"I'm content," said Mr. Harrison. He taught History to boys who weren't up to scratch in the school certificate examinations.

"Won't you take a chair?" asked Father of Captain Sydney, who was still lounging against the wall. But he again refused. He wasn't elderly. He looked wealthy and cared for—a bit of a dandy. He wanted to know if Alan was still at school.

"He is," said Father. "At Derby Hall."

They turned to look at Alan. He wished Madge was downstairs to deflect the conversation.

"How old are you?" asked Captain Sydney.

"Seventeen, sir."

"A difficult age," observed Captain Sydney, and Father flung up his head like a frisky horse, as if to underline the trouble Alan caused.

"It's vital," said Mr. Harrison, keeping his voice low and confidential, "That I should obtain that which I mentioned earlier." He looked at Father meaningfully.

69

"Say no more," urged Father, glancing apprehensively towards the scullery and Mother laying a little white cloth on a tin tray. "Alan," he said. "Go upstairs and look in the box in the blue room. A gold-leafed book. The poems of Swift."

"What room?" he asked. Madge was quite right—with the furniture shifted and the color schemes altered so often, one could never be sure which room was which. Only the sycamore tree stayed in one place.

"Would any of you gentlemen like Daddy's sauce on your cheese?" cried Mother.

"Hurry up," Father said, jerking his head in the direction of the door.

Madge was crouched shivering on the landing. She was cradling in her arms a pair of slippers made out of some red material.

"What are you doing?" Alan asked.

"Thinking," she said.

He opened the wardrobe and felt in the darkness for the ammunition tin that housed Father's spare coppers and documents. He'd been told so often to turn off the light that he'd developed a sense of touch like an animal.

"That blinking wardrobe," said Madge. "It needs throwing out." She squatted in the doorway in her knickers and vest, knees bulging, holding the slippers like a doll. She hated the cabinet covered in green felt. "It looks like it's sprouting grass," she said.

It was one of her annoying affectations to notice textures and shapes. She often disliked someone's hair or the pattern on a teapot, when both appeared unremarkable to anybody normal.

"Get your coat on," he told her. "You're a big girl now."

When they were very little, he didn't know how young, they had listened to the arguments going on downstairs and Madge had crept into his bed for comfort. The rows usually involved Father's business partner before the war or Grandfather's stinginess. Beneath the bitter words came the faint scraping sound of chairs shifting backwards and forwards across the worn lino. "Why are they shouting?" Madge wanted to know, putting fat arms around his neck. "They're not," he said. "They're just talking." They lay under the satin counterpane, scarcely breathing. They played a game. There were three lanes leading to a thatched cottage with a geranium in the window. Through the curtains they could see a table laid with scones and a meat pie. Only one path led to the front door; the others took them into stinging nettles and pig styes. He didn't know how he'd thought up the game. One path went from Madge's arm to her neck, the other across her chest to her armpit. The third path ran down her stomach to between her legs where it was warm and rubbery; they both knew it was the correct route, though they never spoke about it. Madge guessed it was the right path, even though she was little, because she chose it last—like when he ate the crusts of his bread first to enjoy the soft jam centre that remained. It wasn't rude, not really; he hadn't meant any harm. It was just a way of blotting out the angry voices beneath them, the shouting that Bob Ward was nothing but a fifth-columnist, that Mr. Drummond was a mean old bugger. "What's a bugger?" asked Madge. "Why is Grandpa a bugger?" "I don't know," he told her truthfully. "Don't listen. Which is the path to the cottage?"

Alan found the book. It had gold lettering on the front.

"If you ask me," said Madge, "that Mr. Harrison's a bad influence."

"Nobody asked," he said sharply, leaving her on the landing.

Father snatched the book from his hand and slipped it to Mr. Harrison as if he was playing pass-the-parcel. Mr. Harrison bundled it into the pocket of his raincoat.

Captain Sydney was on his way to a gathering in Ainsdale. "A little discussion," explained Mr. Harrison, "on the effects of war on the younger generation."

"Are you a teacher?" asked Mother. She was very keen on education. She'd been to a finishing school in Belgium—the cheapest one available according to Father, who had attended boarding school and left before his learning had hardly started, let alone finished. Mother helped Alan with his French homework; she even knew a smattering of Latin. For all that, she wasn't moved when she heard "Twelfth Night" on the wireless.

"No," said Captain Sydney. "I'm just making a few inquiries on my own account."

Mother told her lurid story of Madge's pneumonia during the blitz and having to choose between death under the dining-room table or lung congestion down the air-raid shelter in the back field. "There was very little difference . . . Oak on the other hand, yellow soil and a bit of corrugated tin on the other."

"We decided on the table," said Father. "No two ways about it."

"It was the damp grass that made up my mind," said Mother. "Wading through those poplars in the dark. And dogs went in during the day, you know, and did their business. It was a torment to me," she recalled.

"I meant damage," said Captain Sydney. "To the emotional life of the child. Fear . . . dreams . . . symptoms of one sort or another."

Mother and Father looked uncomfortable— they took everything personally. There were no other children in the world but their own. Above their heads, Madge started to cough again.

"It's the weather," said Mother, stirring her tea.

"You weren't frightened, were you, son?" asked Father defensively.

"No," he said. He hadn't been. He'd enjoyed the interrupted lessons, the Spitfire on show in the park, the daily convoy of tanks lurching along the road to the shore.

When the visitors had departed, Mother and Father discussed Mr. Harrison's eccentric clothes, the Captain's manly build.

"Fancy calling like that," said Mother wonderingly. "Without a by-your-leave."

"A fine-looking fellow," Father said. "Worth a few bob by the cut of him."

"You could have shaken his hand," reproved Mother, looking at Alan. "I don't know why you have to slouch there as if the cat had got your tongue." But she wasn't really bitter. After a moment she asked: "What does he see in that old fool Harrison?"

"He's no fool, Connie. He may look like the Wreck of the Hesperus, but he's no fool."

She started to laugh then. "When he couldn't sit down because of his gathering—"

"Get away," choked Father, slapping his knee in delight.

"I nearly asked him where it was—"

"I should have offered him one of my poultices," cried Father, the tears running out of his eyes.

•4•

ALAN took the morning off school, to go into town to be measured for his new suit. It meant clean underpants and a vest. He was defiant about the expense involved and the expression on his mother's face when the teachers told her, new suit or not, he was unlikely to pass his examinations. He huddled against the station fence, watching the men in the yard shovelling coal into stiff sacks. The slack glittered under a layer of frost. At this hour there were only a few business men on the platform—Father had dawdled over his telephone calls before leaving the house, and it was gone ten o'clock. In the spring the station was circled by alder bushes and pussy willow; the buds thrust fat and creamy through the palings of the fence. Now the trees leaned inland, ripped by the wind blowing across the bleak uncultivated fields. The rose trees by the Gentlemen's toilet were pruned, black and mutilated, a foot above the frozen ground. It might have been Siberia, he thought, save for the council offices and the red brick houses built in a half-moon beyond the coal yards.

Father was in conversation with the butcher from Tuns Lane—he was retelling the story of the farmer who had raised a pig for him during the war.

"I don't mind admitting," he said. "The laugh was on me. I don't blame the fellow. I paid him a fair price. Connie saved all the scraps in a special bin . . . you might say we paid for its keep."

"There's a lot of expense to pigs," said the butcher.

"All my eye and Peggy Martin," cried Father. "Nothing but a bit of mash and a bucket of peelings. This pig of mine got fatter and fatter. You've never seen such a pig. Then, bless my soul"—he clutched the butcher's arm confidentially, he looked up and down the line as if careless talk costs lives—"It turned out to be a sow . . . It did . . . Would you believe it?" He stepped back to see how his words were received. Abruptly he walked away, then swung, eyes loopy under his homburg hat, to face the butcher—"It's as true as I'm standing here."

His breath drifted upon the air and dissolved above the railway track. He was embarrassing to watch. When the train came in, he raised his hat in farewell and jogtrotted along the platform to the middle coach.

"Terrible fellow that," he told Alan. "Breath smells of dripping."

He settled himself into a corner seat; his lips were purple from the cold.

"Sit up," he said.

Alan did, but he felt it made little difference. He was at an age when his body sprawled and it was an effort to square his shoulders. In repose, his father's face was melancholy—he looked like an undertaker in his somber black coat. He jerked his polished shoe up and down and hummed a little tune. He didn't get enough attention at home, thought Alan.

"Funny about that pig," he said—anything to stop Father bursting into song.

"I paid a moderate sum for it," said Father. "And when the chappie offered to buy it back, on account of it being a sow, I let him have it for the same price. I didn't quibble. You have to be scrupulous in business, otherwise you come a cropper."

Please, thought Alan, don't bring up Bob Ward. Let him rest in peace.

"You see, son, there's such a thing as self-respect. And generosity. Now take your grandfather, he hasn't a generous bone in his body." He leant forward, spreading his fingers as though to number Mr. Drummond's selfish vertebrae. He looked like an undertaker in his somber black coat. He jerked a moment. "Well, it's not use trying to score over anyone. Your Mam and I were only talking about it last night." He smiled; he was tickled pink at the reflection that he and Mother were at last on speaking terms. He looked about the compartment with a gratified expression on his face—as if he'd pulled off a business deal. Outside the carriage windows, the golf course swooped up and down; idle men in check caps and fluttering raincoats stalked the short grass, buffeted by the wind and rain. "Dodgers," said Father, taking exception to the sight. "Swindlers and scoundrels." Mr. Drummond was a golfer.

He sat for a while frowning. Then he said: "Your Mam asked me to have a word with you. It appears money's gone from her drawer. Small sums."

Alan saw that his father's eyes had become grave; he was staring steadily at the white sky trailing like a ribbon beside the train.

Alan heard a long drawn-out sigh and realized it was his own. He felt sick at his stomach. "What money, Joe?" he asked. He was ashamed for the banality of his answer. His father was trying to be fair—he had called him "son." His heart raced at the injustice of the accusation.

"I said I'd talk it over reasonably. No harsh words. All you have to do is confess and tell your mother how sorry you are. It won't be referred to again."

"I never touched any money."

"All my life," said his father, "I've had it rough. Humble beginnings, no education to speak of, a battle to keep me head above water. But I learnt early never to take a farthing that wasn't honestly come by. I didn't borrow and I didn't owe and I never ran up a debt. Abide by that and you can look anybody in the eye." But he failed to meet his son's.

There were explanations in Alan's head—words, denials—but he didn't utter them. What was the use? He hadn't stolen anything because there wasn't anything he wanted. He sat there, heavy with mortification, slumped against the window. He was acutely aware that he was pulling faces. Were he and Father so alike? He tensed his jaw to prevent his teeth chattering.

"Give your Mam her due, she thinks we may be partly at fault. You don't ask for pocket money . . . you're kept a bit short. I don't say it's any excuse, but it may have a bearing."

"I didn't touch any money," he repeated stubbornly.

"You went upstairs last night when the visitors called. And a few weeks back when Mr. D. came, you were snooping about the bedroom. Don't deny it."

"I fetched that book," he said helplessly. "You sent me."

He stared at Father's righteous face turned to the window, the hooded eyes intent on the flying gardens of the suburbs.

"I'd prefer it," Father said, "if you kept that under your hat."

It was, Alan thought, a matter of preferences —of one sort or another. He preferred Father, who preferred Mother, who preferred Madge, who—

who did Madge prefer, he wondered?

"All right then?" said Father, patting him on the knee. "Everything sorted out? You have my word, it won't be mentioned again." And he lay back in his seat, a little pinched about the mouth, and dozed until the train entered Exchange station.

Mr. Sorsky, the tailor, was a Jew who had walked across Russia dragging at his sister's skirts. Barefooted into the bargain. Madge said it was astonishing he hadn't become a shoemaker. He'd gone to school with Father. His workshop was at the back of a building in St. James Street, overlooking the river. He'd been bombed out twice during the war. In the passageway were drawings, charred by fire at the corners, of men in trilby hats and natty suits. At the rear of the premises was a window with a view of a warehouse. Father said the sky looked a mess, full of gulls falling like a blizzard, waiting for the grain to be unloaded.

Mr. Sorsky spilled out bales of cloth, tape measure dangling from his neck. Father weighed the different materials in his hand. Something warm but not too heavy, smart but not flashy.

"Exactly," said Mr. Sorsky.

Nobody asked Alan for his opinion. A dark gray suiting was chosen, with a pale thin stripe. "Double-breasted of course," said Father.

Alan said: "Ronnie Baines has got a jacket with a flap at the back."

"For ventilation, I suppose," quipped Father, and he and the tailor chuckled together as they spun out the clerical cloth and draped it like a toga over Alan's shoulder.

In the long mirror he appeared stocky and bowlegged. His ears stuck out. Was it imagination of did he begin to have a look of Mr. Drummond? The width across his cheeks, the fleshiness of his nose, took him by surprise. Madge too was broad in the face and full-lipped—Mother was dominant.

When the measuring was done—he had, it appeared, immensely long arms and rather short legs—Father and Mr. Sorsky took an emotional farewell. They stood like women, gazing into each other's eyes, holding one another by the shoulders. Perhaps, now they were old, they feared each meeting might be the last. Father blew his nose and the tailor hung his head sorrowfully. They both wore foolish smiles.

Father had one or two business calls to make before midday. They visited a paint firm and he asked to see the managing director. The chit of a girl in the office said he was too busy. Father looked startled at the affront; he threw his visiting card on the desk. In the lift he slammed the wrought-iron gates viciously, descending with shoulders hunched, smarting under the rebuff. At the metal box manufacturer's, Mr. Wilkinson the manager came into the corridor and stood drumming his fingers against the wall. From time to time he took out his watch from his waistcoat pocket and studied it. Father rubbed his hands together unctuously and spoke of his contacts in South Wales. Of mutual advantage to both of them, he implied. The manager nodded his head and continued to tap the tiled wall with restless fingertips. When the talk petered out, he clapped Father on the shoulder, relieved to see the back of him.

"It's been a pleasure," he said, voice over-warm, as if he was praising a child.

Father looked diminished and frail in his bulky overcoat, saying his goodbyes, lifting his hat in the air and backing away down the corridor.

As a treat—though he'd been branded a thief—Alan was taken to the Wedgwood café for his dinner. It was down a flight of steps, next door to the station. The restaurant was painted blue and white, the mouldings of the ceiling picked out in gilt. On the pavement, beyond the swing doors, the women stood draped in black shawls, selling winter flowers.

There was a man with a violin tucked beneath his chin standing beside the buffet table. With closed eyes he played "Only a Rose." The diners kept their heads down and pretended not to hear. Father ordered a mixed grill for himself and a pot of tea. He began heartily but he couldn't finish. He pushed his plate away and leaned back, rubbing at his chest.

"What's up?" asked Alan.

"Indigestion," said Father. "The black pudding's not fresh."

Alan watched his father irritably, sitting there with eyelids fluttering and belly pushed against the white cloth. His mouth was open—even a stomach-ache made him play to the gallery—he was sure everyone was looking at them. He said angrily: "Thanks for the suit, Dad."

"You need one," said Father, struggling upright and pouring himself a cup of tea. "That fellow Wilkinson . . . When I think of what he was before the war—"

"I won't get a good report this term."

"Do you know, when I was a big shot in cotton, that Wilkinson was no more than an office boy. That's all he was."

"I've fallen back in Latin," Alan said.

"He lived in a one-up-and-one-down at the back of Huskinson Street. Now look at him . . . a house on the Wirral—"

"And maths—"

"He hadn't even the common courtesy to invite me into his office."

"He seemed friendly, Dad," Alan said. He felt sorry that it wasn't before the war, the big-shot time, doors opening and secretaries bobbing up and down with respect. Father was a good man, hasty-tempered but just. He had never owed a farthing. It couldn't have been easy, telling Mother he had lost all his money; having to leave his big house and the fruit trees in the garden for someone else to enjoy. All Alan could remember of that time was a toy car with silver headlamps, big enough for him to sit in, that he'd pedalled across a path. Did he really remember it or was it only a photograph in an album?

"Friendly," said Father, striking the table in disgust. "The damned Gauleiter."

"Shall I pay the bill?" Alan asked, beg-pardon smile by habit on his face. He put his knife and fork together neatly and waited while Father struggled to reach the wallet in his breast pocket.

"Here," said Father, stuffing a pound note into his hand. "And mind I get all the change. Don't play any of your light-fingered games with me."

*   *   *

On Sunday Alan wore the Scottish tie Madge had given him for Christmas. The boys made jokes about it as he changed into his cassock. "Where's your kilt?" they cried, butting him in the stomach until he fell over, and the verger told him to behave himself.

The vicar had them all lined up on the cinder path for ten minutes before Morning Service began, gowns billowing like a flock of blackbirds in the bitter wind. He said it would make more of an impact for them to file down the aisle from the front, instead of walking in from the vestry. The girls had trouble with their three-cornered hats. Janet Leyland's curls unwound across her cheeks. She ran squealing toward the bicycle shed and hopped about trying to keep warm.

When the organist struck up the opening notes of the processional hymn, the choir entered the church two by two, the little boys in front, the girls following. The congregation rose to their feet and broke into an epidemic of coughing. Alan and

Ronnie walked a pace ahead of the vicar, eyes lowered, hands clasped in prayer. He had joined the choir when he was nine and was now head boy. As the vicar remarked, his voice was nothing to write home about, but he could be relied upon to attend punctually every Sunday of the year. Madge asked him frequently what he saw in all that hymn-singing and bobbing up and down at the altar steps. He refused to discuss it. Had he done so he would have said it was a place to go, somewhere he belonged—that was all. There were occasions though—on his knees in the candle-lit church—when he shivered with dread as the minister spread out his arms like wings and cried beneath the stained-glass window "Lord have mercy upon us, Christ have mercy upon us, Lord have mercy upon us." Listening to that powerful voice raised in supplication, he thought someone must hear. When younger, it had been his task to work the bellows for the organist. The rhythmical rising and falling of the leather bladder was like the functioning of his own lungs. He pumped desperately, imagining that should he pause and the music stop, then he too would cease to breathe. How could he tell Madge something like that? He did tell her about the treats—the annual outing to Blackpool, summer camp, the mulled wine at Christmas. "Catch me going out with a gang like that," she said scornfully. He never mentioned the weddings and funerals and baptisms, for which he was paid half-a-crown, nor the separate kinds of crying endured in the all-embracing church—babies caterwauling under white lace, bride's mother sniffling into her bouquet of carnations, the hiccoughing grief of the veiled mourners. Sometimes he read the lesson; he had a good voice, loud and unhurried. His mother came once, in her largest hat, to hear him. She talked about it for weeks afterwards. Father rarely attended, which was just as well, with his weakness for bursting into tears. Madge wasn't aware how known he was in the village— a respected member of the community. None of his family realized in what regard he was held.

Halfway through the service, when the choir faced the congregation for the Lord's Prayer, he noticed the German prisoners of war occupying the front pews. Wearing green greatcoats, they stood shoulder to shoulder. In the middle of reciting "Give us this day our daily bread," he saw that a man in the second row wore a white shirt and a plaid tie. He couldn't believe it; the tie was identical to his own. He made eyes at Janet Leyland, who tossed her head. He sat and knelt and stood again, as if in a dream. He jabbed his finger repeatedly in the direction of the prisoners and Janet Leyland wrinkled her brow and looked at him without understanding. The vicar sang "O God make clean our hearts within us," and the choir responded "And take not they Holy Spirit from us." How could a Jerry get hold of a tie like that? He fingered the neck of his black cassock; Hilda Fennel frowned.

In the vestry Janet asked him if he had a sore throat.

"My tie," he said. "One of those blighters had one like mine."

"Is it unique, then?" she said tartly.

"Didn't you notice? The fellow in the front row. The one with fair hair."

"They were all fair," she said.

When he went home for his dinner he passed the soldiers marching down Brows Lane. He twisted round on the crossbar of his bike to look at them. Janet was right: they all appeared the same, arms swinging, coats buttoned up to their chins.

There was pie and cabbage for Sunday lunch. Cutting into the swollen crust, Mother unearthed the upturned cup smeared with gravy. The watery sunshine spilled through the curtains and made patterns on the tablecloth.

He said: "We had those Jerries in church this morning."

"Oh yes," said Mother.

"The vicar wants us to forgive." He laid down his knife and fork. "Some of us have forgiven them already."

"I don't hold with it," Father said. "When I think of the sacrifices our Russian comrades made."

"There was one bloke in particular . . . with a long thin face."

"It's their families I feel sorry for," said Mother. "Worrying . . . not knowing where the poor lads are."

"Don't talk rot. They write home regularly."

Madge picked at her food and said nothing.

"I'd shoot the lot of them," said Father. "If it was my choice."

Mother said Madge had been down to the woods all morning, looking for tadpoles.

"She'll have a long look," said Alan. "This time of the year. Doesn't she have any homework to do?" He wanted to jump up and shake the truth out of her.

"Leave her alone," flashed Mother. "She does her best."

*   *   *

That evening, Alan confided in Janet Leyland; he had to tell someone. They whispered together in the bicycle shed—he didn't want Ronnie Baines to hear.

"Good heavens," said Janet. "What a worry for you."

"I don't know where to turn," he confessed.

"I've seen her in the village once or twice. Dressed in trousers, without shoes."

"They're my cast offs," he said. "She runs wild."

"Don't her feet get cut?"

"What am I going to do?"

She thought for a moment. "You ought to tell your Mum."

"No," he said. "I oughtn't."

"Well, you'll have to catch her red-handed, then."

88

"It's pitch dark," he said. "I don't know where she meets him."

"Did she really see Cyril kissing Hilda Fennel?"

"I'm not concerned about Hilda Fennel," he said.

"Perhaps you should go to the camp, then, and complain."

"I can't be sure," he told her, "that she's meeting anyone. You never know with Madge. Sometimes she likes you to think she's up to something and she's not doing anything at all."

Janet seemed disconcerted. In her woolly scarf and her knitted hat she stood a little apart from him. "You'll have to catch her with him, in that case. Then you'll be sure, won't you? You ought to tell him she's under age and things."

"In the pitch dark," he said again.

"He might act violent," Janet told him. "There might be a spot of bother." She sounded as if she'd be disappointed if there wasn't. He thought gloomily that if it came to blows he would take to his heels.

"What a way to behave," said Janet. "I think it's disgusting."

"It doesn't do," he said, "to jump to conclusions." And he walked away from her into the porch, feeling he had been disloyal to Madge. Even if she was meeting a blithering Jerry down on the shore, she was probably only chatting to him about God.

He never enjoyed Evensong as much as Morning Service. There was no dinner to look forward to; the congregation was sparse. Sometimes the mist rolled in from the sea and filled the body of the church; the old ladies shuffled like gray ghosts behind the pews and coughed forlornly. He wouldn't look at Janet. He felt she had let him down.

Later, when he was backing his bike out of the shed, she approached him and said she was sorry —she hadn't meant to upset him.

"I'm not upset," he said.

She wanted to help him if she could, for Madge's sake as much as his own. It bothered her, a young girl like that, getting up to heaven-knows-what mischief.

"We could go now," she said. "Down to the shore."

"Now?"

"It's not late, Alan. It would take a load off your mind."

She rode on his crossbar as far as the round-about; the wheel of his bike wobbled under her weight.

"You'll have to walk up the hill," he said.

She talked to him about her friend Moira and her cat Mitzi. Under the sulphur lamps the pom-pom of her hat seemed to catch fire.

"She's got a lovely sense of humor," she said.

"Mitzi?" he asked.

"No, silly. Moira. She's got a crush on you."

He had no answer to that.

Janet went to the Isle of Man every summer for her holidays. It was nice there in the summer

—her Mum and Dad and her uncle Arthur.

"It's wizard," she said. "You'd love it. We go on excursions and things. I don't half miss her, though—"

"Moira?" he said.

"Me cat, you clot," she cried, striding up the hill, her hands in her pockets. She had a robust laugh, like a boy's; he thought her a little bossier than when he first knew her.

From the top of the hill the sky showed pale against the black line of the woods. The night was stormy; the trees rocked against the station fence —even the lighted windows of the scattered houses seemed to flicker like candles. Few people lived this side of the railway track. The land was given over to the sea. A few cows might graze in an exceptional summer, or a horse be put out to pasture, but mostly the earth lay swollen with rain-water. It was the reason for Madge's cough, Mother said—the everlasting dampness and mist rolling in from the shore.

When they swooped down the hill he kept his hands clenched about the brakes; Janet screeched in the face of the wind. Beyond the barn used by the Scout troop, the lane narrowed between the waterlogged fields, the ditch ran underground. The street lamps ended. They turned the corner into darkness. He slowed down.

"I can't see anything," she said. She was whispering.

"Wait on," he told her. "After a bit it gets lighter. Look up at the sky."

The clouds raced above the arched lattice of the elms.

"Is that the sea?" she asked, listening to the murmur of the pines pulled by the wind.

He laid his bicycle behind the wall of the cemetery and led her down the path between the graves. Through the iron railings a light shone in the porch of the vicarage; the church had been derelict for as long as he could remember. Janet clung to his arm. She stumbled over the roots of ivy and gave little chortles of laughter as if someone was squeezing her in the darkness. He trampled the brambles underfoot and pushed open the wicker gate. Their feet sank into the pile of wreathes left rotting by the fence.

"I don't like this," she said, stopping stock-still.

He was filled with protectiveness towards her. She was so foolish, so clumsy.

"Haven't you been here before?" he asked.

She thought it was a criticism. She said defensively: "In the summer. In daylight."

He took her hand; in its woolen mitten it lay in his like the paw of some animal. He guided her down the avenue of pines. The north side of the woods grew on a ridge of high ground above a shallow valley of sand and star grass. Frogs bred in the pools of rainwater, beneath the alder bushes and eucalyptus. Beyond the valley the sand dunes stretched to the edge of the shore. To the east the trees covered the land for two miles, from the dunes to the golf course, dense and hardly penetrable.

"My Mum and Dad," said Janet, "would never let me out in the dark. Are yours daft or something?"

He couldn't see her. All that joined them were her fingers and her side pressed to his as they jolted through the trees.

"You don't know Madge," he said. "You can't tell her anything."

He had almost forgotten they were looking for his sister. They were climbing the ridge now; the pine mulch underfoot gave way to wet sand. They were out of the trees and on to the rise, overlooking the valley.

"Oooh," she wailed, spun in a circle by the unleashed wind.

She wanted at once to retreat into the shelter of the woods; she was frightened to go alone. He was elated by the wild agitation of the bushes below, the gale tearing through the topmost branches of the pines. Far out, he heard the faint muffled boom of the buoy at sea. He hadn't been there for years; he could understand now why Madge felt compelled to go out every night.

"Isn't it grand?" he shouted, clothes flapping, arms spread wide as though he might fly.

Janet whined and complained at his back. She was cold. She couldn't bear it. Reluctantly he went into the woods. Away from the winds, his cheeks smarted; he had ear ache. He huddled on the ground and Janet wound her scarf selflessly round his head. She fussed over him and scolded.

"I'm all right," he protested, dragging the

scarf away and leaning against a tree.

She sat beside him, an arm about his shoulder. He didn't think it was affection so much as fear of being in the dark.

"We'll never find your Madge," she said.

"I'm not bothered. I don't think she's up to anything. You see, it's very cramped at home, very confined—"

"Cramped?" she said.

"There's not much space. All cooped up in a little kitchen. It can get on your nerves."

"Haven't you got a lounge, then?" she asked.

It was useless trying to explain that the lounge was kept for visitors.

"Can you see any normal man," he said, "Jerry or otherwise, meeting our Madge on a night like this? She wears ankle socks."

"It must be cramped for him," she said. "Confined behind barbed wire. And beggars can't be choosers."

Such perception made him uncomfortable— just as he was beginning to dismiss the whole business from his mind.

Janet rubbed his ears with her gloved hands. He thought he'd like to kiss her. She almost lost her balance; they stayed a long while in an awkward position, mouth to mouth. The trees sighed all around them. She broke away from him and searched the ground.

"My hat's come off," she said. "My Dad bought it for me."

"Here," he said, feeling the wool under his hand, spiked with pine needles.

"What does your Dad do for a living? He's on the train at funny hours."

"He's in commerce," he said.

"What's commerce, then?"

"Dealing and things," he said. "He's a socialist too."

"He ought to be ashamed," she said, snuggling closer to him. "My Granddad was a liberal. He used to live with us before he died. Is your Granddad living?"

"Yes," he said.

"Does he live with you? Is that why it's so cramped?"

"No," he said. When the blitz was at its height, Mr. and Mrs. Drummond had come to stay with them. It was supposed to be for the duration, but after two days Father got into a paddy about lumps in the porridge and his grandparents left. Then Father said Aunt Nora should have a chance of survival and she stayed a week. When she went she said she preferred the bombs to the continual bickering.

"Is your grandmother alive too?" she asked.

He wished she would stop talking and let him concentrate. He was touching the front of her coat, trying to push his hand between the buttons. For warmth. The coat wouldn't allow it. He found her knee and shoved his hand under the thick material; she wore so many clothes. At her waist, beneath her jumper, she was wearing a satin underslip. Below that was a vest—he could feel it with his finger and thumb. He almost gave up. He couldn't put his hand under her skirt. It was too rude. He wanted to, but he couldn't be sure of her reaction. Partly it was the darkness, not being able to see her face. She wasn't saying anything; perversely she had fallen silent. He was on his own, heaving her about under the slender trees, trying to get comfortable, clutching her by one bulbous knee.

She said: "Don't . . . please don't."

He was irritated. He hadn't done anything. Ronnie hadn't either, or Peter Jeffries. Ronnie had been smiled at by a land-girl a year ago, but it hadn't come to anything.

"Mother would be cross," Janet said.

Her mother, whom he had seen in the village and at church, was apple-cheeked and big-hipped. She wore a little straw hat with faded curls pushed underneath.

"Beg pardon," he said, taking his hand away. He strained his eyes, looking through the pines toward the ridge, wondering what the time was.

"My Uncle Arthur did that," she said. "I've never told anyone before."

He was astonished by her. He didn't know what to say. He didn't hold with that kind of talk.

She was kneeling now, struggling with her clothes, stretching her arms up and wriggling. When she sat back she felt for his hand and held it tight. He understood she wanted him to kiss her again. He leaned foorward, searching for her mouth, but she was lifting his hand and guiding it to her chest. She'd unbuttoned her coat and her jumper was rolled up to the armpits. She shuddered at his touch.

"It's all right," she whispered. "Your fingers are freezing."

She wore a boned brassiere with little bits of frilly lace. He dug for her skin and was amazed at the warmth of her.

"Don't pinch," she said sharply.

He didn't know what it was leading to, this fumbling in the darkness. He tried to remember the verses about the waaf and the sailor, but they all dealt with bottoms and knickers and he wasn't allowed there. He thought of a jumble of things he had learned at school, fertilization, rabbits, cross-breeding—it had nothing to do with the way he felt now, the bursting in his head, the congestion lower down. She was like a rubber ball; he couldn't get a grip. Her breasts bounced away from him. Blow this, he thought, taking his hand away and putting it in his pocket. She was upset he could tell, but she didn't say anything. He wanted to tell her it would be all right in the summer when it was warm and fragrant and her clothes weren't so bulky. It was the thickness of her vest, the sensible stockings, her hat and gloves, that put him off. She was more like a female relative than a sweetheart.

"We ought to go," he said. "Your parents will wonder where you are."

"They won't," she muttered. "They'll think I'm at the youth club."

"Well, mine will. My Dad gets annoyed."

She stood then, leaning against him for support, brushing the needles from her legs.

"You're an odd family," she said, settling her hat more firmly over her ears.

He thought that was a bit much, considering what she had told him about Uncle Arthur.

She was silent along Brows Lane. She was petulant by the Grapes Hotel. At her front gate she hung her head and seemed about to cry.

"I'm off," he said, losing patience with her, and he rode away, whistling under the street lamps, despising her. It wasn't fair, blaming him for not knowing what to do. If he had known and he'd tried to do it, she wouldn't have let him.

Madge was sitting on her own in the kitchen. Mother and Father had gone to the Bay Horse for a drink.

"Did you go out?" he asked.

"No," she said. "You've got pine needles in your hair. You want to be rid of those."

He flushed, but he went on to the back path to rub his head. He felt peculiar; he had a pain in the pit of his belly. He wandered down the garden to beyond the greenhouse and sat in the damp grass facing the poplars. In the past, when he had been in disgrace with the family, he used to go into the front garden and lean against the sycamore tree for comfort. Then Mother built a rockery around the base and painted the stones with white emulsion; he was forbidden to step on the plants. So many things were forbidden—he wondered if Janet Leyland would speak to him again. She was probably at her friend Moira's at this very moment, telling her every detail.

He tugged in misery at the grass and something moved under his wrist. It was a carrier bag half-buried beside the holly tree. He pulled it free and felt inside, touching something made of rope or string. There was a torch in the greenhouse and he took the bag and tipped its contents on to the bench Father used for his tomato cuttings—he counted five pairs of sand shoes, rope-soled with red canvas tops. Across the toecaps were serial numbers stamped with indelible ink.

He went indoors and called Madge into the scullery.

"Leave them alone," she cried. "I hid them."

"What do you have to hide shoes for?" He couldn't think why she was making such a fuss.

"They're not shoes. They're slippers."

He looked at the numbers on the toe caps. "And what's that in aid of?"

"They're made out of army mail bays," she said. "They stamp everything . . . so it doesn't get pinched."

He stared at her. "Why on earth do you want them?"

"I don't want them. I'm selling them for a friend." She heard footsteps coming up the path. She rammed the slippers into the potato bag under the sink. Mother and Father were back.

They'd met Captain Sydney at the Bay Horse. Wasn't that strange? He'd paid Mother a lot of attention.

"He's rather nice," she said. "Pompous, but rather nice."

"He looked barmy to me," said Madge.

"He commented on my hat," said Mother, pleased.

Father acted proud. In another kind of mood

he might have taken offense. He looked at Mother in admiration—she wore her chic little hat tipped forward over one eye.

"I'd say he was quite dazzled," he said. "No two ways about it."

Mother had been dazzling, once before, to a business colleague of his. Father caught him pecking at Mother's cheek in the back of the car—he saw them in the front mirror. He stopped the car on the main road just outside Ince Bludell and pushed the man into the ditch. He lost his agent's commission but he said he didn't give a dicky bird.

"Come in pet," he called to Madge, who was hovering in the scullery. "You'll catch your death."

They sat for a little while drinking tea by the fire; they were a happy family.

Father promised to take Mother into town during the week and buy her some sort of bracelet.

"What's the occasion?" she cried, eyes sparkling from her gin and lime.

He said he just felt generous. He'd give Madge ten shillings while he was about it. After all, Alan had his new suit.

Mother went upstairs and ran the bath water. She bathed every day, while Father managed it once a fortnight.

Father rinsed the cups and after an interval followed Mother upstairs; he was going to loofah her back.

With her parcel of slippers, Madge ran down the garden and returned out of breath, her socks wringing wet. Directly she sat down she began to cough.

"Shut up," Alan said. "You turn it on like a tap."

"I can't help it. I've got a tickle in me throat."

"There's nothing wrong with your throat," he said bitterly. "The specialist never found anything."

"Nothing physical," she snapped. "I didn't have a shadow on my lung, but he did ask me if they ill-treated me."

"You make me sick," he said. He was thinking of the ten shillings Father was going to give her.

"The trouble with you," she said. "You keep everything bottled up. You won't face facts."

He wouldn't answer her.

"Take your suit," she said. "You didn't want it, and yet you went like a lamb to be fitted. You never stood up for yourself."

"You took that new costume at Christmas," he said. "And that velour hat with the feather."

"I didn't wear it, though. I've never had it on."

She was right. No matter how Mother raved and stamped her foot she refused to put on the purple costume and the tyrolean hat.

After a moment she said. "There'll be trouble over that Captain Sydney. You mark my words."

It was an expression of Father's. He couldn't help smiling.

"I don't trust Mr. Harrison," she said. "He's a dirty old man. Any friend of his is up to no good."

"Don't talk daft."

"He lends Father dirty books. I read one. It was all about somebody doing wee-wees in chamber pots."

101

"You've a wonderful imagination," he said.

She grew indignant. "It's the truth. It was that book you got out of the ammunition tin. It was—"

"They were poems—"

"About wee-wees and Stella making rude noises."

He laughed out loud, though he didn't like her talking of such things. Above their heads, they could hear Mother chuckling in the bathroom.

"Hark at them," said Madge. "It's the only time she lets him near her . . . when he's going to buy her something."

"Be quiet," he said.

"She shaves down there, you know. I've seen. She must think she's an artist's model."

"You want to wash your mouth out," he cried in a fury, jumping to his feet and slapping her knowing pink face.

He got told off for his pains. Father leapt downstairs and belted him over the head. He went to bed in disgrace.

·5·

SEVERAL weeks passed during which Janet Leyland established herself as his girl friend. Every day when he came home from school she contrived to be waiting for him on the platform. At choir practice and the club she attached herself to him like a shadow. She was always at his elbow, smiling, picking up the ping-pong balls, fetching him cups of tea. She stopped being bossy. When he looked up from his hymn book she was observing him tenderly. Her skin was so delicate that the least touch left a pink spot, slow to fade. He was flattered and bewildered by her attentions and not sure that he cared to be taken over so completely. His friends teased him, but he knew they were envious.

"I didn't think," said Ronnie. "That you'd be the first. Not with your family." Mrs. Baines encouraged him to go to dances and was always chiding him for not yet courting. He asked Alan what he did with Janet.

"Kissing and that," he said.

"Anything else?" he wanted to know.

"Give over," he said. "What sort of a question is that?"

He stopped larking about with the boys after church. They went to the pictures together once but Janet Leyland came too and nobody really enjoyed it. There was a constraint between them. They couldn't talk as easily with her sitting there clasping Alan's hand tightly for all to see. She made a face when he jumped over the seats to buy an ice-cream.

Mrs. Leyland turned the gas fire on and let them sit in the front room of an evening. When nine o'clock came she brought in a little tray with tea and biscuits.

"Thank you very much," he said. "I don't want to put you to any trouble."

In the beige room with the neat furniture and the three-piece suite, he might have been at home. Mrs. Leyland thought he was very polite, very much the college boy. She told Janet his family were well-to-do, owning a car and everything. She would have liked to question him personally, but was too reticent. She sipped her tea with them and Janet sat between the two people who were now sharing her life, important and languid, occasionally laying her hand on Alan's sleeve and casting a fleeting triumphant glance at her mother. Then

Mrs. Leyland sighed and collected the dishes to go into the kitchen to her husband. Now it was settled they were going steady, Janet didn't expect him to behave in a demonstrative fashion. They spent a fair amount of time kissing and squirming on the leather sofa, but she never put his hand on her chest. It satisfied her that they were seen to be courting—when they walked in the village she linked his arm as though they were a married couple. He turned his head away and whistled as if he was indifferent to her.

Moira called once to sit with them. Janet leaned her head on his shoulder and stared sleepily into the fire. The cat lay across her stomach like a small black rug. He didn't think it was true that Moira had a crush on him; she didn't speak directly to him nor would she look at his face. At first she spoke in an animated breathless way about the blouse and skirt she was making in needlework at school. It was blue and white and her teacher thought it very stylish.

"The blouse has a Peter Pan collar and pearl buttons," she said.

"That's nice," said Janet.

"The skirt is sort of fitted, with a pleat here and another at the back." She stood up and ran her fingers down her hips to show what she meant. She wore her reddish hair tied back with blue ribbon, exposing large, highly colored ears. Alan couldn't help noticing her legs. "I've been making it for four weeks now. I can't wait to get it finished."

"It sounds lovely," said Janet. "Doesn't it

sound lovely?" The cat jumped down from her knee and she was now stroking Alan's neck with one cold little finger.

"Yes," he said, jerking his head away.

"I saw your mother tonight," said Moira. "At the station."

He thought at first she was talking to Janet. "My mother," he said. "Do you know her?"

"She wears very smart clothes," said Janet. "You can't mistake her."

"You can," he said firmly. "She never goes out at night, unless she's with my Dad."

They fell silent then until Mrs. Leyland came in with the tray. After a short while Moira said she must go home. There was a lot of whispering in the hall before the front door was opened.

Janet returned to stand pensively on the rug, staring down at the fire. "You like her, don't you?" she said.

"She's all right."

"Do you like her better than me?"

"Don't talk silly. I hardly know her." He didn't think it suited her, being so childish. It was all right for Madge to pout her lips and bow her shoulders —Janet looked like her mother, head on one side, corkscrew curls tipped over her ear.

"She's spiteful, you know. She's played some nasty tricks on me."

He knew he should say something to reassure her, but he couldn't be bothered. He had a little picture in his head of Madge sallying forth into the garden with her watering can. He was sat half-asleep in a deck chair. She poured a thin jet of water down his sock. Did Janet mean that sort of trick? Or throwing those verses belonging to the school prefect down the lavatory? He sat for twenty minutes, not talking, reading the newspaper that someone had left on the fireside table. He sensed that Janet was watching him. She lay across the carpet, stroking the stomach of the cat and crooning into its fur. He stood up finally and stretched his arms above his head. He waited for her to say goodbye, but she didn't move. So he let himself out thinking if she felt like that she could lump it. She followed him immediately and clung to his arm as he maneuvered his bike down the path.

"I'm sorry, pet," she said. "Don't be angry."

"I'm not angry," he said reasonably, mounting his bike and riding away.

She ran after him. He knew she was chasing him—he was afraid to ride too fast lest she should lose him; but then he didn't want her to overtake him. It would be too cruel to get clear away. Never before had he been the cause of such a scene—he was consumed with guilt and excitement. At the Grapes hotel he had to wait while a vehicle drove out of the car park; in the public bar they were cheering over a darts match. Her footsteps pursued him along the pavement. She seized his arm and almost pulled him to the ground.

"Don't be stupid," he said, looking at her face blotched with misery.

He saw tears in her eyes and the melting outline of a cheek against the dark background of the street. He couldn't continue with his show of bravado. He dropped his bike with a clatter into the gutter and patted her shoulder remorsefully.

"I'm not worth it," he said wisely. "You don't want to let me upset you."

"What was it about?" she asked, the tears running down her face.

He didn't know. It was probably something different for her.

"You will see me?" she pleaded.

"Tomorrow," he said. "Of course I will."

He didn't walk her back up the road because he thought her mother might be watching from the window. Instead he stood at the curb, waving his hand encouragingly as she shuffled up the street in her slippers. He couldn't help thinking he was like one of those shepherds making signals to a collie dog, herding sheep into a fold.

*　　　*　　　*

His suit was half-finished. It was a reminder that he was that much nearer the day of the school meeting, when his progress would be discussed. It was like the dentist—the date was chosen and nothing short of death would cancel the appointment. It soured his days and made him sleep badly. He woke in the night, eyes wide open in fear, the room going round and round as if he were fainting. He saw very little of his family. When he came in from the Leylands he went straight up to bed or did his homework in the front room; he'd stopped asking his mother for permission. Sometimes Madge was missing and Father would be stamping about on the front porch, muttering and blaspheming. He presumed relations between his parents were again strained, as Mother was usually in bed when he went upstairs. The light was on, but he didn't say goodnight, because he never had. It would have been admitting some kind of guilt if he had called out on the landing that he was there, that he was home. He had to keep up his pretense of detachment.

One night Father caught him in the scullery preparing a cheese sandwich. He'd thought he was safe and that Father was keeping his vigil for Madge under the sycamore tree—but Father had sneaked up the side path and rushed through the door, catching him with the bread in his hand. Father spat with fury. He got down on his hands and knees and picked up the crumbs one by one from the string mat and hurled them into the fire.

"Do you think it's a blasted hotel," he shouted.

"I would have brushed them up," Alan said. He wiped nervously at the marble slab in case the margarine had smeared.

"You'd do nothing," Father bellowed. "Nothing. None of you do a blasted thing." He was throwing the carving knife into the sink and turning on the tap with such force that water splashed up the sides of the bowl and hit the wall.

"Keep your voice down, Joe."

"I'll shout in me own home. If you don't like it, clear off out. Let your Mam go off too with her fancy man if she likes. I'll be glad to see the back of her. She can go to that wonderful family of hers—"

Alan watched his father. Another word and he might have struck him. He felt hatred for a moment. He couldn't bear the sneering mouth, the mean forehead lowered under the dark blue beret.

It was all Madge's fault—giving her ten shillings hadn't made a blind bit of difference. He left his sandwich uneaten on the plate and went into the kitchen. Father followed, rushing forward at a great pace to seize the poker from the hearth. Alan started back—he thought his father had gone mad —but he was only bending down to rake the fire. He muttered savagely under his breath, ugly sounds that petered out into a low groan of pain as he stood upright and cracked his skull on the mantle. Alan would have helped him then, but Father blundered away, nursing his head, and hid like a wounded beast in the dark scullery.

Miserably Alan went upstairs. He heard his mother calling. She was propped up in bed reading a library book.

"What was that all about?" she asked.

"I dropped some crumbs," he told her. She made him feel shy, lying there with her glasses perched on the bridge of her small nose, her mouth still red with lipstick. Something in his voice touched her.

She said: "Don't take any notice, Alan. Just ignore him."

"Why can't he control himself?"

"Don't take any notice. Is the wireless on?"

"He ought to get himself seen to," he said.

She looked at him with pity. "Don't let it upset you. It's not worth it. He's a rotten old man."

It made it worse not better. He cried out: "Leave him alone . . . he's hurt himself."

"Come here," she said gently, patting the bed.

He wouldn't go to her. He stood with averted face, looking at his grandfather's photograph on the chest of drawers.

"What's all this I've been hearing about you and some girl?" she asked. Her voice wasn't angry.

"Where did you hear it?" he said.

"Mrs. Cartwright in the fish shop mentioned it. I felt a bit of a fool not knowing what she was talking about. The girl's in the choir by all accounts."

"Yes," he said.

"Well . . . go on . . . tell me about her. Is she nice?"

"She's just a girl," he said.

"Wouldn't you like to bring her home?" She didn't look at him. He imagined her mouth trembled as she waited. She said: "You've every right, you know. You're not a child."

He wondered if she was waiting to participate in his life, seeing she had none of her own. Would it make her happier? She had no wrinkles on her face that he could see, no traces of the difficult years she had lived through. Her eyes had a bright bland look behind the cheap spectacles.

"I don't mind," he said. She was so anxious to please, he wondered if he dare mention that he wasn't doing so well at school.

"Well," she said. "You choose the day and let me know when she's coming."

"What about my Dad?"

"Don't fret yourself. I'll handle him." She was quite pink in the face with satisfaction. She jettisoned her book on to the floor and clapped her hands so childishly that he couldn't help smiling.

*   *   *

They chose a Saturday lunchtime for the visit; it was unusual but it was the day Father spent most of his time in the garden, hoeing the frozen ground and raking the stones from his vegetable patch. It wore him out and made him more tranquil.

Mother behaved with generosity. Dearly as she would have loved Janet to see the dining room, the silver and the cut glass arranged on the sideboard, she understood that Alan would prefer it if they ate in the kitchen without fuss. She made Father a cup of tea at eleven o'clock to mollify his temper; he raised his eyebrows at her gesture. There'd been an incident the night before about a telephone call which Mother took and said was a wrong number. Father said she was a blasted liar, just like Mr. D. She shut her ears to him, refusing to go white and mute up the stairs; she was too busy making a cake for Janet Leyland. Madge wasn't in to lunch. She was down at the shore. It was just as well because there wouldn't have been room for them all round the table. Before Janet arrived Mother took hold of Alan's arm and said he was a good boy. He was ashamed of the tears that came unbidden to his eyes. He shook her off and continued to open the tin of condensed milk.

"I won't go on about it," said Mother. "But I appreciate you replacing that five shillings in my drawer." She went and fetched her purse from behind the wireless. "It was too much," she said. "Only four shillings went missing." And she pressed a shilling into his hand.

What could he do? She thought he'd stolen and she thought he'd put it back. One denial cancelled out the other. He was richer by a shilling for not doing anything.

Janet chatted about her cat and her holidays in the Isle of Man, which was a much nicer place than anyone ever thought, and really everyone ought to go there sometime. Of course her Dad had been born there, but that didn't mean she couldn't see the wood for the trees.

"And what does your Daddy do?" asked Mother. "In business, is he?"

"He's in the Bank," said Janet.

Mother raised her eyes in surprise—it was more than she'd hoped for.

"She's rather pretty," she said kindly when

Janet went upstairs to wash her hands. Father grunted a lot and curled his lip. He wasn't impolite but there was an edge to his remarks. Mother gave him several severe glances which he took meekly enough.

"I want to do something with animals when I leave school," Janet said. "But you need a lot of qualifications."

"Really?" said Mother. "You do surprise me." She was thinking of Mr. Riley who kept ferrets down the road and a gray whippet that he'd once entered for the Waterloo cup. Alan hoped she would keep her mind on animals and not dwell on future careers. Usually she told everybody at the drop of a hat that he was going to be a Town Clerk —as if it was something you fell into quite accidentally, like a hole in the road.

Janet had two helpings of steak-and-kidney pudding out of politeness. "I love steak and kidney," she said.

"I can see that," said Father, and he laughed sardonically and stuffed the food into his mouth. For once he had kept his teeth in—he was making some effort. Mostly he put them in his handkerchief at the commencement of a meal. It made Madge ill; she said he was ugly and insensitive. "It's only me blasted teeth," he would cry, champing his gums to annoy her.

At the end of the meal Mother suggested they might like a cup of coffee. At this, Father, who had been eating a piece of cheese, flung his knife on the cloth and sat back so abruptly that he caught his shoulder on the overhanging wireless.

"My word," he sneered. "We are grand. Been getting a few ideas from our military friends have we?"

Nobody knew what he meant. Mother took no notice; she hummed a little song as she waited for the water to boil. Janet helped to carry the dishes to the sink. It was something his father normally did, not out of duty or habit but because he thought no one else could do the job properly. Madge said he should have been a parlor maid, the way he fussed over the scouring of pans and the polishing of the cutlery.

Janet didn't know where any of the plates belonged, so she stood in her wool dress, arms folded, and remarked on the prettiness of the garden beyond the window. She'd been to the hairdressers; her curls ran stiff as cardboard over her rounded head.

"It's a terrible lot of work," said Mother, looking at the swampy lawn and the dormant branches of the rambling rose.

Trailing his rake behind him, Father walked slowly down the path to the greenhouse.

Mother took Madge upstairs to show off her jewelry and her hats in the wardrobe. Madge never paid any attention to such things. Alan could hear his mother, shrill with delight, opening drawers and cupboards above his head. He thought it odd that women of whatever age were so similar in their ways, loving clothes and babies, forever going on about friends and relations and prices of materials. Madge was the exception. You wouldn't catch Madge spending an afternoon trying on hats and admiring a string of beads.

As he was dozing by the fire, he became aware of someone peering in through the curtains at him. It was Father, come to see if the tidying up had been done properly. He rearranged several plates on the scullery shelves and then scrutinized the kitchen floor for scraps. He needn't have bothered; it was only Madge who dropped her food in an abandoned manner. As he searched, his behind caught the edge of Grandfather's chair, tumbling the arm to the rug. It was too much for him to bear. He ran to the back door and hurled the offending piece of wood clear over the privet hedge on to the lawn. Alan stood at the window and watched him race after it—he kicked out; the wood slithered even further down the garden. He was like a demented saboteur swooping down on a faulty hand grenade, lobbing the curved arm towards the trenches where the vegetables grew.

At the greenhouse Father paused and spun round. Alan ducked and scuttled to sit at the kitchen table. He was glad Janet Leyland was upstairs playing milliners with Mother. Father came in and seized last week's newspapers from behind the bread bin; he took a packet of candles from the pantry. He was breathing heavily. All his gestures were grandiose and liberal. The ironing board was knocked to the floor. He didn't seem to care about the mud he was trampling into the scullery mat. He still ran, as if walking might slow down his sense of purpose. Disappearing behind the green-house, he emerged finally, minus his newspapers, one finger held up in the air as if he asked for silence.

It's rum, thought Alan, not knowing what he should do. Father was obviously going to burn the arm. Whatever would Mother say? He tried sitting experimentally in the chair to see what difference it would make, and even though he knew what to expect he banged his wrist on the pegged upright of wood that was now exposed. It was dangerous—trip over the hearthrug and you could lose an eye.

As he sat there, mentally listing the accidents that could happen, Father came at him like a mad-man. Gripping the lapels of his school blazer, he dragged Alan out of his seat and flung him into the scullery. Father was manhandling the chair out of the kitchen, over the mat and on to the path. He was trying to carry it down the garden.

"What are you doing, Joe?" Alan cried, strug-gling to pull the furniture away from Father; he was hampered by the thought of Mrs. Frobisher next door seeing them. He relinquished his hold and went back indoors. The chair, with its lumpy cushion and padded back, was heavy; Father's legs were buckling as he passed the pagoda. Somehow, lurching and pursuing a zig-zag path across the sodden grass, he managed to reach the green-house. There he dropped his load and bent over, clutching his side. His A.R.P. beret fell to the ground. After a moment he dragged the chair out of sight.

The kitchen looked odd without it. The lino was dusty where it had stood. A tennis ball and a knitting needle lay in a wad of fluff against the skirting board.

"Mum," Alan called.

"Won't be a minute," she answered.

But she was half an hour. By that time there was a strong column of smoke rising into the air beneath the populars.

"Go into the lounge," said Mother. "I'll put the kettle on."

Janet whispered how lovely his mother was, what hats she owned, what jewelry. "Trays of it," she said.

"Yes," he said. "She's a great hoarder."

It was all cheap stuff he knew, because she'd told him: costume jewelry from the Bon Marché, paste diamonds sparkling like the real thing but not worth insuring.

"She's charming," said Janet. "You're lucky." And she sat wistfully on the sofa hugging herself for warmth, admiring the polished desk and the watercolors framed in gilt on the white walls.

He couldn't sneer at her; they were both alike, saying the right thing out of ignorance or good manners.

Mother couldn't understand why he wouldn't take Janet home after tea. He said curtly, "You best go on your own," and Janet stood up and fetched her coat without a word.

"You'll take her home surely," rebuked Mother, distressed at his lack of gallantry.

"It's quite all right," Janet said meekly. She trembled at his indifference and his mother's regard for her feelings.

"I can't go out," he said. "I'll see you at the club this evening."

"After your piano practice," snapped Mother, turning spiteful.

He couldn't look out of the window for fear the whole sky was darkened by the black smoke from Grandfather's chair.

"She's a very nice girl," said Mother, when Janet had been waved down the road. "Very sensible."

He thought maybe it was a criticism, and he thought she was possibly justified. But on the credit side, sensible girls wouldn't lapse into moody silence or burn possessions out of spite.

"Look," he said, taking his mother to the window. "He's made a bonfire."

After all, there was only a thin scribble of smoke like a pencil mark drifting above the greenhouse. Mother hadn't noticed the absence of the chair, but when he told her she was out of the back door before he had finished his sentence, running down the garden with the panel of her dress floating behind her. He followed, anxious for them all.

Mother swore at Father. She called him a twisted old bigot. "What harm did it do you?" she cried, as though speaking of a domestic pet, looking at the charred remains of the fireside chair and wringing her hands in misery. "How could you?"

"Shut your trap," shouted Father, leaning on

his rake. The embers of the fire glowed as the wind swept through the grass.

"You've no right," she said, high and bitter, rubbing her goose-pimpled arms. "It was an antique."

"It wasn't worth a brass farthing," he countered. "He couldn't give it away, the mean old bugger."

"You'll end badly," said Mother. "By God, if there's any justice, you'll end whimpering."

"Please," pleaded Alan, "come on in," and he tried to take her arm.

She pushed him away and advanced upon Father, fluttering her hands and demanding, "What did your family ever give you? They never had two pennies to rub together . . . what did Nora ever get out of life?"

"Leave my sister out of it," warned Father, raising his rake like a weapon.

"You wouldn't let her have a life of her own in case it interferred with your business. Bob Ward might have married her if you hadn't put your oar in—"

"Don't mention that damned fifth columnist."

Father spat with anger. His cheeks wobbled as he tried to find words. Something fell from him and landed in the fire. Sparks eddied upwards into the trees. He clutched his mouth and Mother turned away in disgust. Alan knelt and groped in the warm ashes for the dentures. As Mother ran back up the garden, she began to laugh. She trotted over the wet grass and went squealing behind the privet hedge; the sound of her laughter carried across the bleak and desolate gardens.

"It's all right," said Alan. "Here they are."

He wiped the pink gum on his coat and handed it to Father. He knew why his father had false teeth—he'd been told often enough. Lack of vitamins, poverty, neglect. Father was fed, in his day, on bread and potatoes, and if he had tooth-ache he either wept or was taken to the paupers' hospital, where the dentist in the butcher's apron dragged out the molar by brute force, and left him bloody in the chair. Rationing and nutritional planning had changed all that.

Alan went into the house to find Mother. She'd put herself out to make the day a success— the cake, and the little paper napkins tucked under the plates. The chair had burned because she had spent time being nice to Janet Leyland. She wasn't in the kitchen. Alan stood on the landing and listened to her sniffling inside the bedroom.

"Mum," he said. He hoped she wouldn't hear.

"Go away," she wailed. "Leave me in peace."

He put on his overcoat and went into the front room to do his piano practice. He had such chilblains that he stopped playing several times to scrape his fingers against the edges of the keys.

*   *   *

Alan met Madge at Exchange station after school, to take her to visit Nora. It was their Aunt's birthday. Mother had given Madge money to buy a potted plant and a box of hankies. Selflessly Madge gave him the hankies so that he wouldn't arrive empty handed.

He didn't like the town at dusk—the ruined buildings that dwarfed the hurrying people, the damaged statues tilting on cracked and monumental pedestals in the square. He could see Queen Victoria on a chair of stone, dumpy and offended under the lamplight, knees shattered and the coiled hair on her neck silvery with the droppings of gulls. His own mouth drooped in ill humor as the office workers rushed homewards along the pavement, buffeting him as they surged forward under the glittering strands of the overhead cables and broke like a wave to cross the street. He hated standing there with Madge, flamboyantly raising her eyebrows in expectation, making a show of herself, searching each face in the crowd as though she looked for someone in particular. When the tram came rattling down the hill, she clapped her hands like a child at a party, gazing in wonder at the fizz of blue sparks that spat into the night sky.

"Stop it," he hissed. "Behave yourself."

She leapt aboard the tram, not listening, and parked herself on the long bench with lips parted like a movie queen, glancing about theatrically, her shoes swinging clear of the floor and her laces trailing in the dust. She was desperate for attention. He dug his elbow sharply into her ribs; but she smiled, sly and wayward, fixing her eyes on the old woman seated opposite, calling out above the clatter of the tram as it accelerated up Argyle Road, "We're going to visit my Auntie. It's her birthday."

The old woman tittered, swaying in her seat, trying to avoid Madge's bright and beady eye and drawn back every time, until she was forced to ask: "Your Auntie, is it?"

"This plant's for her." Madge held up the pot swathed in brown paper. There was a crackling sound, like fire, as she unwound the stiff wrapping, revealing a small fern with corrugated leaves, thin and weakly. She lifted it up for all to observe. "Did you ever see anything that pretty?"

Alan wished her in hell, making an exhibition of them both. His cheeks burned at such exposure. He sat upright on his seat and felt afraid. The company he chose for himself afforded security—he could predict reactions—with extroverts like Madge or his father he was continually pitched into situations of danger. He was trapped like a rabbit on a country road, mesmerized by the headlamps of murderous cars, waiting to be struck down.

The old woman was standing on the platform ready to alight. The driver dragged on the brass handle of the brake and the tram shuddered to a halt beside a blitzed acre of ground.

"Tarra," called the old woman, stepping down into the gutter.

In the pockets of darkness lay the bomb-sites, rubble overgrown with tall and multiplying weeds; the wind blew constantly from the river, scattering the dust and the seeds across the demolished city. Father said the high explosives had blasted the plants out of the granite rock beneath the town. In summer, between the twisted girders, in fields of brick the purple flowers bloomed. It wasn't natural.

The tram started again; the hammering of his heart became less urgent. Cruelly he took hold of Madge's arm, pinching the skin so that she winced and drew away.

"If you say another blithering word," he warned, "I'll get off and leave you."

She sulked but stayed silent. It wasn't that she was bothered at being left alone—it was what Mother would say if he told on her.

Aunt Nora lived in a rented house in Everton Street. She paid thirteen shillings a week for the cramped dwelling and the slateyard at the back with the wash house she never used. Father stored papers and old clothes in the wash house—he couldn't bear waste. In a carrier bag was a child's suit with a tattered lace collar that he'd worn at a school concert when he sang "Lily of Laguna."

At the end of Nora's street stood a Chinese laundry.

"I love the smell," said Madge, wrinkling her nose.

She was romancing as usual. The laundry was closed, the soap suds rinsed clear down the drains. He could smell nothing save for the stench of tomcats issuing from the mouth of the air-raid shelter.

Aunt Nora was busy making sandwiches. She

said she was expecting friends for a little celebration. He thought she must mean the lady next door. She kissed his cheek, holding him tightly against her flat chest, telling him he was a lovely lad to bring her hankies.

"Is my Dad fetching us?" he asked.

"Search me," she said. "He's in a right paddy these days."

She let Madge make tea and butter the scones. Alan read the newspaper and struggled not to yawn. He was fond of his aunt, he might almost have loved her, but despite himself whenever he entered the mean little house with the ugly patterned wallpaper and the curtains stained lemon with age, he wanted to fall asleep. His aunt never minded. He lay on the sofa and dozed against the cold and musty cushions. He could hear Madge chattering on about home and the chair that had gone up in flames.

"Sheer foolishness," said Nora. She was out in the back, washing dishes.

"I never liked it," said Madge. "There wasn't room to turn round."

"He never had such a temper when he was a lad," observed Nora. "He's grown mardy."

"When he was little," asked Madge, "was he quiet, like our Alan?"

He didn't approve of the way his aunt confided in Madge. She was too free with her talk. Anything she said would be round the village in no time; Madge didn't hold with secrets.

After some time he heard Nora say, "Your

Mam demands too much. She drives him too hard. Expecting this, expecting that. What's the poor devil to do?"

He wanted to protest. He muttered into the cushions: "Mother sent the handkerchiefs. She told us to come and see you." Nobody heard him. His mouth left a wet stain on the satin cover. He was like an animal hibernating for the winter—curling up his limbs he buried his head deeper into his arms. They were emptying a drawer full of photographs on to the table. He'd seen them all before—seasides, gardens, outings of long-gone relatives—himself in a pram squinting into the sunlight with open mouth, bald head fragile under a cotton bonnet.

"Those bathing costumes," screamed Madge.

"We thought we were bobby dazzlers," tittered Nora.

The two of them at the table broke into different kinds of coughing, Nora wheezing and asthmatic, his sister barking like one of those dolphins illustrated in the geographical magazines.

"Your Dad," said Nora. "He never knew what hit him."

"People choose," Madge said, daft as always. "It's not random."

"He was engaged to Annie Mud," Nora said. "For seven years. I had Bob Ward. We went to Blackpool."

That fifth columnist, he thought, with the oiled quiff of hair and the rounded collars, dead but not forgotten. Someone had told him that the departed only crumbled to dust when they were no longer remembered by the living. Bob Ward must be lying fresh as a daisy in his wooden box.

When he woke he saw Father was in the room, standing in the kitchen doorway with Nora. He was saying, low and urgent, "But it doesn't suit me to have you hand over just yet."

Nora replied tartly, "That's a pity, I'm sure."

"I can't see what ails you," said Father. He was trying to be controlled.

"It makes for bad feeling. I can't stand your Connie giving me the cold shoulder."

"Don't talk soft, woman."

"And she's within her rights. It's not good for relatives to come between man and wife. You sign the whole caboodle over to her. Get her off me back. I don't want the aggravation any more."

Father moaned and cried bitterly. "God damn you, Nora. I thought better from you."

He stood under the center light in his hat and coat. As Mother aged, she grew round and rosy, encased in a warm layer of fat that obliterated the young woman under the cloche hat in the family album. Father was shedding his flesh, paring away to the bone beneath, letting the skeleton emerge. He ground his teeth with passion. He could never be on an even keel—he was either elated or depressed; he knew of nothing in between. He thumped the table with his fist. Nora held her ground.

"It's best," she said stubbornly, and walked out of the room.

Alan closed his eyes, retaining the image of his father's corpse-like countenance, white and shrunken above the knot of his silken muffler. For a long time Father stood there; the sound of his breathing filled the room. Then he went into the hall. From the front parlor came the noise of voices singing and the jangle of the untuned piano. The front door slammed. Alan sat up and brushed the fluff from his clothes. Aunt Nora returned with a stack of plates.

"So you've come back to the land of the living," she said, smiling at him.

"Where's Dad gone?"

"Home," she told him. "He wasn't feeling too good. He's not well, Alan. Your Mam should make him see a doctor."

"There's nothing wrong with him," he said, shaking his head irritably.

"He gets pains in his chest."

"He eats too much," he said. "He always has."

Alan wouldn't join the party in the front room. Madge was sent through to persuade him but he refused. "We're levitating," she said. "We sing 'Shall we gather by the River' and someone goes right up in the air."

"I'll bet," he scoffed.

"Mrs. Enright went up two feet. She might have gone higher but she was worried about showing her drawers."

"My Dad's been and gone," he said. "Auntie says he's not well. He ought to see a doctor."

"He eats too much," she said carelessly. She

looked flushed and happy, he hair ribbon hanging in a bedraggled bow above her ear. He told her they ought to be going soon, it was getting late.

"I want to stay," she whined. "Why can't we stop the night? Mother wouldn't mind."

"I'm not stopping here. It's too damp. There's not the facilities."

"Silly old Alan," she said. "You're scared of everything." And she would have kissed his cheek, only he fended her off; and she went with a pretence of huffiness to join the old ladies rising in the front room.

She was right: he was scared—but not of the damp. He was afraid of leaving his parents alone together in the house. He had to be sure Mother was in the upstairs room and that the car was parked on the path. He needed to be certain Father was sitting safely by the fire, listening to the voices in the dark.

On the tram journey to the station, Madge said she reckoned she knew what all the check-signing was about. "Auntie told me when you were asleep."

"I never slept."

"Our house belongs to me and Auntie. In our name."

"She's no right to gossip," he said.

"It's family business . . . not gossip."

"She ought to have more sense."

"It's to stop Mother spending all the money on hats and things."

"Shut your mouth."

"He's bankrupt. He can't have things of his own."

"I don't want to know," he said. "You keep your lies to yourself."

It was raining; the streets glistened under the street lamps. Along the dock road the cobblestones would be slippery under the wheels of the big car. He ought not to have let Father go home alone. During the war they had come back one night from visiting Aunt Nora and the sirens had begun to wail behind them. Father cursed, putting his foot down hard on the accelerator, trying to put distance between himself and the town. Through the back window Alan watched the bloated fish of the barrage balloons, sliced in half by the pale beams of searchlights. The car skidded on a patch of oil, and a pound of apples, lodged in the front compartment, burst their paper bag and cannoned about the seats.

Though the war was over, Father was still caught in a crossfire, harrassed by battles, by phantom cities tumbling about his ears. This moment— as then—he could be slumped over the driving wheel, hands raised in an abject gesture of surrender.

On the train, Madge said loudly. "Have you ever thought how many clothes our Mam buys? All those cotton frocks and handbags to match."

"Shut up," he cried. "She has a right to her dresses. What do you know?" And he glared at her so fiercely that for once she had no reply and stayed mute on the upholstered seat opposite him, looking down at her lap.

130

When the train drew out of Hall Road station, he imagined she stared more intently into the darkness. They ran along the coast now, swaying beside the golf course and the invisible sea.

"Looking for the camp, are you?" he asked bitterly. She annoyed him so. "Still chasing Jerries are we?"

"I don't chase," she said. "I don't have to. You don't know anything about me."

She was near to tears, her face red and her mouth wobbling. He stopped goading her then; he didn't want a scene in front of the other travellers. When it was their stop she ran ahead to the door and darted away down the platform. She ran headlong up the steps, the belt of her raincoat trailing behind her. He waited till the train had gone and crossed the line by the wooden planks inside the tunnel. It wasn't allowed but there was no one to see him. When he climbed the ramp he thought he glimpsed Madge on the other platform, hovering behind the ticket box. He waited a moment, fearing she would follow him and anxious for her safety. But he had been mistaken. He walked between the coalyards and the bicycle shed towards the road. How silent the village was compared with the town. He could smell the damp grass, the sharpness of the sea breeze; the privet hedges boxing the front garden showered his shoulder with raindrops. At the corner he was almost blinded by the headlamps of a car driving at speed. The car braked and he heard his Father calling out furiously— "Alan, where's your Mam?"

He ran to the window and stared in stupidly. "Where's Madge?" he asked.

"Don't give me lip," shouted Father. "Have you seen your Mother and her fancy man?"

"No," he said. "I haven't." And he cowered away from the car and his father at the wheel, denying all part in it: the man was bankrupt. The car drove on.

Alan called all over the house for Madge, thinking she was hiding to pay him out for talking about the Germans. He undressed for bed and sat in the dark at the top of the stairs, waiting for someone to come home. After a long time the car came back and was left parked in the street. He got into bed then and put his head under the covers. Shortly afterwards he heard Madge return and Father bellowing at her.

She came upstairs and went into the bathroom.

"Madge," Alan whispered. She didn't answer. She was making a humming noise as she brushed her teeth.

"Madge . . . is Mother back?"

"Shut up," she said. "I'm not talking to you."

He ran from the bedroom and seized hold of her on the landing. He shook her so hard the toothbrush fell out of her hand on to the carpet, smearing the pile with paste.

"Look at that," she whispered, kneeling in her knickers and vest to rub it away.

"Where's Mother?"

"How the heck should I know?" she said.

But he thought she did know; she was too un-concerned. Defeated he lay in the darkness, listening for Mother's footsteps on the path.

At last she came. He held his breath ready for the outburst of violence. It was too late to turn on the wireless to fox the neighbors.

Doors closed, water ran in the sink. Nobody shouted. A knife clattered on the draining board—Father was fixing himself one of his little snacks. He heard the swish of Mother's clothes as she climbed the stairs. She murmured something to Madge, who began to cough mutedly as though she buried her face in the pillow or in Mother's arms. Father stayed silent downstairs—in the kitchen that wasn't his, in the house he didn't own.

A LAN told Janet Leyland nothing of his mother's nightly disappearances, nor of his father scouring the neighborhood in the car. Coming after his disclosures about Madge's wanderings in the dark, he feared her sympathy. She would think them all barmy, going in different directions, playing at hide-and-seek. When he thought about it from an outsider's point of view, he almost smiled. It was so different at the Leylands, everyone sitting down together at the supper table, talking normally, lapsing into comfortable silences when there was nothing left to say. He thought they must find him difficult to get on with. He made an effort to seem at ease; he had a way of tilting his chin that gave him an air of gravity and confidence. It fooled Mrs. Leyland. She fussed over him, handing him dishes and apologizing for her dulness. When her husband left the kitchen to sit in the front room, she said: "You must excuse us Alan. We're not clever folk. We don't know much." He nodded in a matter-of-fact way and sat on stolidly at the table, unable to contradict her. Sometimes Janet stood behind him and linked her arms about his neck. She leaned on him. He stayed very still, embarrassed by such a demonstration in front of her parents.

When they went on an excursion together, Janet paid the expenses—the tickets, the cup of tea in a café. Father had forgotten his promise to give him pocket money and he didn't like to ask.

They met Madge one afternoon by the railway crossing, on her way back from shopping for Mother.

"I'm his sister," she said cheekily; he hadn't thought to introduce them.

"I know," said Janet. "I've seen you in the village."

"Ah well," Madge said, and she prowled in a circle round them, clutching a loaf of bread and grinning.

"Where's your shoes?" he asked crossly.

"In the hedge. What's it to you?"

Janet smiled self-consciously—she kept her arm linked proprietarily in his.

"Is she coming home for tea, then?" asked Madge. "My Dad's not in."

"What's that got to do with it?" he said, frowning. "She can't anyway . . . she's got things to do."

136

Madge wouldn't give up. "Do you know our little plantation weed?" she asked. "Our little Joe Stalin?"

Janet was bewildered. "No," she said, looking at Alan enquiringly.

"Come on," he ordered, tugging at her arm. "You've got things to do."

"I'm helping a friend to make a dress," Janet said.

"What a kind girl," cried Madge. "I do like helpful people. It does make the world spin more smoothly." And she ran off ahead of them, the soles of her bare feet showing black with dirt.

"Is she very clever?" asked Janet.

"She's batty. She needs a thundering good hiding." And he said goodbye to Janet on the corner and walked home quickly to give Madge a piece of his mind.

Madge had climbed the sycamore tree. She was throwing lumps of bread on to the path. "Stop that," he shouted. "Your hands are filthy."

He told Mother what she was doing. "My loaf," cried Mother angrily, and was heard shouting on the porch for Madge to get down. After a few moments there was laughter; Madge had got round her. Mother came into the kitchen holding the mutilated bread, exclaiming fondly: "She's a little twirp."

"She's too bold. You're not firm enough."

"There's no harm," she said. She didn't seem to realize how wayward Madge was, what danger she might be in.

"I know different," he shouted. He was knotted up inside with anxiety.

"It's grim enough in this house," she retorted. "You ought to be glad she's not worn down by it." She'd been at home all day, pottering about the garden. She wore a faded blue dress and a handkerchief tied about her hair. When she laughed she stopped looking tired and frowsy; her chin doubled and a little dimple appeared in her cheek.

"Look at that bread," he cried furiously. "Look at the state of it."

Madge came in, holding her shoes in her hand; she'd ripped her jumper on the tree. She said mildly: "We're not deaf, you know, Alan. You don't have to raise the roof."

He pointed his finger accusingly at the wrecked loaf. It wasn't the bread he wanted them to look at; it was everything that was being torn apart. After tea Madge would clean her teeth and set off for the shore. She would be out for hours in the dark and nobody seemed to care.

"It's more mangled than that," said Madge, "when it's in your stomach. It turns into blotting paper."

"I couldn't touch a crumb of it," he said.

"Well, don't touch it, swallow it," she said, and Mother laughed out loud.

Madge sat on the floor where the chair had been, leaning against the wall and stretching her legs out across the rug. She didn't seem to notice that Mother had to step over her every time she went in and out of the pantry. Mother didn't mind;

138

she trotted down the garden to bring in the washing. She stopped a few moments on the path to chat to the lady next door. Alan was told to switch on the light. The clock in the hall chimed five o'clock.

"Shift yourself," Mother bade Madge, a shade irritably. The color was going out of her face; it would soon be time for Father to come home.

"When I was up the willow tree," said Madge. "I could see a bird's nest in the guttering."

"Oh dear," exclaimed Mother, fearful for the drain pipe.

Alan thought Madge was possibly making it up. She saw things that she wanted to see. "Why can't you call things by their proper names?" he asked her. "It's not a willow. It's a sycamore."

She didn't look at him. She said, "I didn't think you liked to call things by their proper names."

They heard the car revving up the path. Mother turned on the wireless and closed the curtains. She seemed to grow older. After a few bars of music a man's voice began to sing. "Night and day, you are the one." Father put his key in the front door. Suddenly Madge was crying; she sat with the tears rolling down her cheeks. Mother looked at her in dismay.

"Whatever's wrong, pet?" she asked. She knelt awkwardly on the floor and pulled Madge to her. The voice on the wireless sang—

"Only you beneath the moon and under the sun . . . Whether near to me or far

Darling, makes no difference where you are . . .
I think of you Night and Day
You are the one."

What a noise Madge was making, gasping and opening her mouth in a long-drawn-out wail of anguish as though her heart was breaking.

"What's wrong?" asked Father, coming into the kitchen. He'd removed his hat and there was a red mark across his brow. He stood distraught, looking down at Mother swaying back and forth on her haunches like a native woman.

"She just burst out yelling," said Alan. "She was all right before." He had to bite his lip not to mention the mess she'd made of the bread.

"She's growing," said Mother tenderly. "Poor little pet."

She told Father to light the gas under the potatoes and stop gawking at the child. He was so grateful at being included that he never made a murmur about the washing left on the draining board.

It wasn't like the last time, when Madge had broken down to deflect anger at coming home late. During the meal she had difficulty swallowing her food, but she tried, for Mother's sake. She wasn't putting on an act. Her face was washed out, miserable; her hands trembled when she reached out to drink her tea. Once, when Mother had sprained her ankle and they phoned for the doctor, Father flew into a rage at the sheets on the bed. He'd put a wet bandage about Mother's foot

140

and carried her upstairs like a child, but the sight of the crumpled bedding sent him into a fury. "Do you want the doctor to think we live in a slum," he shouted, jerking the sheets from under her swollen foot, making her hop around the room, fetching pillow cases, changing the counterpane. But he wasn't angry now; both his parents seemed to know it was serious. They talked quietly and calmly, trying to repair the damage.

"Madge says she saw a nest in the guttering," said Mother.

"I'll look at it tomorrow," said Father reasonably.

"I cut the hedge."

"That's good," he said. "It needed a trim."

They were very polite. He mentioned he had dropped in on Nora. "I found her pretty sprightly," he said, as though he had not seen her in years.

"That's nice," remarked Mother, with an effort.

They watched Madge leave the table. They didn't know what to do for the best. Alan followed her. In the hall he asked her not to go out. "You look peaky and it's raining."

"It doesn't matter," she said listlessly.

"They won't row tonight," he promised. "I'll stay in too if you like."

She was putting on her coat. He couldn't help remembering her telling him about the specialist who'd asked if she was ill-treated.

"It'll pass," he said awkwardly. "You can't be

expected to understand what it's like for Dad
. . . trying to get business . . . going round begging
for orders."

"I don't know what you're talking about," she
said. "It won't pass. He's going away." Her eyes
were filling with tears.

"Who's going away?"

"I love him," she said. "He's going away . . .
back to Germany."

He could feel the anger rising in his throat. It
wasn't that she was too young or the disgrace of
going with a Jerry—it was the word "love" that
choked him. He hated her using the word.

"Do you realize," he said, "only a few years
back you would have had your head shaved?"

She took no notice. She was squashing the old
panama on to her brown untidy hair.

"What about our Mam and Dad?" he demanded. "You'll be the death of them."

"Them," she said contemptuously, going
out of the door into the rain. "What do they
care?"

*   *   *

Aunt Nora telephoned the house later in the
week. Alan spoke to her because Mother was upstairs.

"Shall I get Mum?" he asked.

"No," said Nora. "Hold on lad." There was a
pause.

142

"Who's that?" shouted Mother from the landing.

"It's Auntie."

"Well, take your shoes off. Tell her your father's not home yet."

"My Dad's not home yet," he told his Aunt.

"I know," she said. "I've left him on the sofa. He's had one of his turns."

"Turns?" he said.

"He's not well, Alan. He's nervy. You tell your Mam to get him to a doctor."

"All right," he said.

"I liked me hankies, love. It was thoughtful of you."

"Yes," he said.

Mother had been listening in the hall. "What was that all about?"

"It's Father. He's not well."

"Really," said Mother. She examined the floor in the front room to make sure he hadn't put dirt on the carpet, and went back upstairs with an offended expression on her face.

Alan told Madge about the phone call. She sat at the table with a little smile on her face.

"What's so funny?" he demanded.

"I'm upset," she said. "I suddenly had a feeling that it's true. Him being ill. It's nothing to do with him eating too much."

She stared down at the cloth. He knew what she meant—you could go on for years imagining that illness happened to other people, and then it was near you, right in your own family. If Father ate so much, why was he so thin? He didn't take any exercise apart from the garden and hosing down his car.

"There's a girl at school," said Madge. "Her mother died. She was right as rain one moment and the next she was dead. The daughter wasn't allowed to go to the funeral."

"Stop it," he said.

"She couldn't cry. She knew her Mam wasn't coming back but she couldn't help grinning."

She was beyond him. Half the time she made everything up. "Auntie's probably got it wrong," he said. "She exaggerates things." He wanted Madge to confirm it, but she said nothing.

When Mother came downstairs Madge told her to sit down and she'd make a cup of tea.

"What for?" asked Mother. "You're very helpful all of a sudden." But she sat back in the remaining armchair with her head resting against the cushion and closed her eyes. Her pinny was splashed with paint; she'd been giving the trap door into the loft another coat of whitewash.

Madge drank her tea on the floor, cocking her little finger in the air to please Mother. The house seemed quite silent, Mother breathing gently, the cup and saucer balanced on her stomach.

Madge said: "You ought to take Dad to the doctor's."

Mother's eyes snapped open. "Ought I, Miss? And what do you know?"

"Has he ever been ill before?"

Mother tossed her head. She didn't care for

Madge being worried about somebody else. She always wanted the attention; if there was any concern going begging, it ought to be for her. "Ill," she scoffed. "Him? Never."

"Did you ever like him?" asked Madge, relentless.

Alan had the delusion that if he kept very still at the table, they would think he had gone away; he crouched there over his cup, face turned to the window. The room was darkening. In the house next door they had switched on the downstairs light.

"He was thought very well of, in the old days," said Mother. "He had a future. But he was spoilt as a child. His sister ruined him. He was sent away to America as a boy."

"America?" said Madge astonished.

"For his health. He went as a cabin boy on a sailing ship. Of course he's years older than me."

"A sailing ship?" said Madge with wonder. "Golly."

"It was years ago," Mother said irritably, sensing Madge would go on and on. "Long before my time."

It seemed odd to Alan. He'd only been as far as the Lake District. He'd had three knife-and-fork meals in a restaurant in all his life. Janet Leyland hadn't had one. "What was he ill with?" he asked, thinking of his Father before the mast, the wind blowing and danger on every side.

"How the heck should I know?" said Mother. "I doubt if there was anything wrong with him. He was cossetted from the moment he was born."

"But he was poor," said Madge. "He didn't have much schooling."

"Don't talk like that," cried Mother, and she got up and collected the cups, her mouth set in a thin line of annoyance. It was like swearing or telling a rude story, mentioning poverty. It wasn't nice. She went into the scullery and slammed the dishes into the sink.

"I'd have thought," said Madge cunningly, "it was in your interests to make sure he's healthy. If anything happened—"

Alan was horrified by her. He thought Mother would come through and clout her one. Instead she came into the kitchen and asked him: "What exactly did Nora say?"

"He's had a turn." He couldn't see her face; the room was too dark.

"What sort of a turn?"

"I don't know," he said. "She didn't say."

"I'd like to be a cabin boy," said Madge. "It's not fair. I can't do anything."

"You could join the tennis club," snapped Mother. It riled her that Madge wouldn't wear shorts and white plimsolls and have a social life. "I was never off the courts at your age . . . in Belgium, at my finishing school. We had a garden when your Father and I were first married, big enough for a game of tennis. We had a maid called Matty. We had so much space . . . You have no idea what it was like." She stood by the hearth, one foot resting on the cracked tiles.

146

"We've got space now," said Madge from the floor. "You won't let us use it."

Alan thought suddenly it was why Madge went out so much, why he did himself. There wasn't room for them. If he had his way he'd light a fire every day in the lounge and lie full-length upon the good-as-new sofa.

"Father had a pain," he said. "When we went to Mr. Sorsky's for a fitting. His mouth looked blue. He thought it was the black pudding."

"Blue?" said Mother.

"It must be tiring," Alan ventured, "traipsing round town, calling on people."

"He spends most of his time at his sister's," said Mother scornfully. "Flat on his back on the sofa. She's soft as butter with him."

They had their supper and Mother didn't save any potatoes or gravy for Father. She was cheerful, talking to Madge about the way she'd been sought after as a girl, the education Mr. Drummond had given her.

"How did you meet Father?" asked Madge.

"On the top of a tram," replied Mother, but she wouldn't tell the whole story. Perhaps she no longer remembered. She never said anything that made you sit up—she was very technical. She had been going to visit her cousin—it was a No. 22 tram. She wore a gray coat with a side-fastening and pigskin gloves.

"How did you know it was love?" persisted Madge. "When you first saw him?"

It was embarrassing. Alan wanted to shout out

that she was a stupid beggar. Of course it wasn't love. Didn't Mother confirm that every time she opened her mouth?

Mother recounted some story about a party she'd gone to when Father turned up on the doorstep and caught her with another beau. "His face," she recalled. "It was a picture." She and Madge began to laugh at this image of Father foolishly standing in the hall, holding his hat nervously in his hands, knowing Mother had deceived him.

"What happened?"

"Father left," said Mother, and they both doubled up over their plates, smitten by the comical aspect of the occasion.

Perhaps Mother had bewitched him, or maybe, contrary to what she implied, she had thrown herself at him. He was well-to-do in business. He was engaged to Annie Mud. Hadn't he travelled across the world?

At that moment Father came home. He walked up the side path and entered the kitchen while they were still laughing. He stood, blinking under the light, a look of reproach on his face. He was waiting for Mother to wonder how he felt.

"Are you all right?" asked Madge.

"Mind your own blasted business," he said, and he stalked into the hall, slamming the door ineffectively behind him.

"He seems all right," said Mother. "In his usual cheerful frame of mind." And she and Madge stuffed their hands against their mouths and tittered.

Alan stood up when Father returned with the evening newspaper. It was an empty gesture because he knew his father wouldn't care to sit at the table and be one of them. All the same he pretended he didn't need his chair any more. He leaned against the wall and fiddled with the knob of the wireless.

"You're messing the curtains," said Mother. "Stand up straight."

Father went into the scullery, looking for his meal kept hot in the oven. He came savagely to the doorway, demanding: "Where's me tea?"

"I didn't think you'd be well enough to eat," replied Mother.

She winked at Madge. She was unaffected by him. His harsh voice and bullying ways hardly bothered her. Of late she had grown detached and thoughtful, as though she had something else to think about. It must have been different, thought Alan, on the No. 22 tram. Otherwise he and Madge wouldn't be here now.

*   *   *

The next day Madge somehow got round Father and persuaded him to go with her to evening surgery.

"I'll come too, if you like," offered Alan.

"You're mighty concerned all of a sudden," sneered Father, but they could tell he was touched.

He wouldn't admit he'd been poorly at Aunt Nora's. Mother pretended she didn't know where they were going, but she made Madge put on a clean blouse and change her socks.

The surgery was in a large house set back from the road, with chestnut trees in the garden. The interior had polished wood floors and deep windows overlooking the lawn.

"Lovely building," said Father, getting up to examine the moldings of the door.

There were several people that Alan knew, sitting in the waiting room. Mr. Hennessey from the bowls club stopped to have a word with him. "Are you playing in the match this Saturday?" he wanted to know.

"I expect so," Alan said.

"Do you think we're in with a chance, then?"

"Could be," he said.

Mr. Hennessey sat down on the opposite side of the room and Father whispered: "Who was that?"

"Chappie at the church."

"Playing what?"

"Bowls," said Alan shortly.

Father looked at him amazed. "Do you play bowls?" he asked. "I thought it was for old men." And he leaned forward on his seat, dangling his homburg hat between his knees, shaking his head in wonder. He knew very few people to talk to in the village. He didn't mix much. He said it was a question of economics. He hadn't the money to waste on being social. Alan thought the reason was his temperament and his daft views. He was too emotional and there wasn't exactly a vast body of sympathizers waiting to share his interest in Joe Stalin and our glorious Russian comrades.

"You tell the doctor everything you feel," said Madge, leaning close to Father. "Tell him about being on a sailing ship."

"Get away," said Father. "What's that to do with it?"

"You have to give the whole picture," she said. "It's not just now, you know. You can have things wrong with you from way back. Or nothing at all. There's people who can't walk and there's nothing wrong with their legs. This girl at school, her mother—"

"Shut up," hissed Alan. Mr. Hennessey was looking at them.

· "There's nothing wrong with my legs," said Father, pushing Madge away from him. "It's pains in me chest."

"Well, tell him how irritable you are most of the time."

Father jerked upright. He was about to bellow that he wasn't blasted-well irritable, but he thought better of it. The quietness of the room, the rustling magazines and the muted coughing deterred him.

When it was his turn to see the doctor, he marched away leaving his hat and gloves on the seat. At the doorway he collided with a woman just entering. He stepped backwards, apologizing profusely, bowing from the waist. He tucked his hand

151

under the woman's elbow as though to steady her. She smiled and turned quite pink in the cheeks.

"He's not like that at home, is he?" whispered Madge.

"None of us are," Alan said crossly. He went over to sit with Mr. Hennessey and disregarded her completely. She fetched a magazine and stuck her thumb in her mouth.

"Who's that?" asked Mr. Hennessey, looking at Madge sitting there like a big soft baby. "Your sister, is it?"

"No," he said, praying Madge would leave them alone. It infuriated him—talking about love one moment and behaving like an infant the next. That blinking Jerry, if he existed, must have a screw loose somewhere, to be bothering with Madge.

Father was a long time in the surgery. When he came out he looked paler than before, as if contact with the doctor had brought on ill health. He jammed his hat on to his head and told them to hurry up.

"We should have brought the blasted car," he said. Madge hadn't let him; she implied he didn't take enough exercise and walking would do him good.

"Well, what did he say?" asked Madge, hanging on to his arm.

"He's got connections with a man I know in South Wales," said Father. "He comes from Cardiff."

They were walking up the road toward the

Council offices. There was a slight drizzle of rain drifting down from the darkness.

"Did he examine you?" asked Alan. Maybe Father was being brave. It was unlikely, but perhaps he was keeping the truth from them.

"I'm as sound as a bell," said Father. "Just a bit overworked, which is something your Mam would never give me credit for. He's given me a prescription for some pills—"

"For your heart?" said Madge.

"Get off," he cried. "Coloured paste for wind."

It was a bit of a disappointment, Father being fit as a fiddle. It would have been easier to put up with him had he been suffering from a medical complaint. Immediately Madge became her old awkward self. "I'm off," she said. "I think I'll go for a walk."

"You won't," argued Father. "You'll come home with us."

She would have run off, but at that moment, under the lamps at the roundabout, Father gave a queer strangled cry, as if he was choking. He stopped stock still and clutched his chest. He was staring at a man hurrying along the road toward the station. He said: "It's that damned scoundrel. It's him."

He looked as though he was going to faint. They had to help him to the bench outside the park gates. He slumped there like a bag of bones, his black hat tipped over his eyes.

"What's he on about?" asked Madge. She

looked helplessly at Alan. She peered down the road and said again. "What are you on about?"

Father wouldn't answer.

Alan had seen him too—Captain Sydney in his overcoat with the velvet collar, heading for the station steps.

It was too cold to stay on the bench long. Father's teeth were chattering.

"Help me home with him," said Alan.

"Do it yourself," she said defiantly. "I'm off." She walked over the road. At the privet hedge she called out, "He's playacting, Alan. The doctor said there was nothing wrong. Don't let him trap you."

Alan held Father's arm and led him slowly down the street. They walked on the wet strip of grass beside the park, so that if Father fell he wouldn't hurt himself. When they reached the house, it was in darkness. Mother had gone out— she hadn't even waited to know how Father was.

Alan took Father's hat off and eased him out of his coat. It was as well Mother wasn't in—there would have been nowhere to sit. He poked up the fire and asked if he should fetch a sip of brandy. There was some kept in the front room, for the visitors who were never invited.

"I can't afford it," said Father wearily. "Just get me some water."

He dipped his nose into the glass like a bird. He had a little dab of color on his cheekbones now. He said. "You know where she's gone? To meet him."

"Don't be daft," Alan said.

"Yes, she has. You saw him. Madge spotted her at the station the night you came back from your Auntie's. She meets him there."

"I don't believe it," Alan said. He didn't know why, but he didn't think his mother would bother. She wasn't made like that.

"Where's she gone then?" demanded Father. "The only time she's ever gone out at night was with me or to her dressmaking classes."

"It's Madge you should be worrying about," said Alan. "She needs guidance."

"Your Mam's never walked out of the house before. Not night after night. Not without saying where she was going," persisted Father.

He wasn't interested in Madge. He should have been—she influenced them all without their knowing; she peeled back the layers. She had only to hint it was a trap, that they weren't a close family, and it was a fact. She was contagious. If she hadn't begun to go out in the first place, worrying everybody, leading her own life, Mother mightn't have copied her.

"Maybe," Alan said, "she's still going to the dressmaking. She doesn't let on—to annoy you." It was Madge talking again.

"It's ten years ago," said Father. "When you were babies." He grew maudlin. His voice trembled. "She made all your clothes . . . little frocks for Madge . . . shirts for you."

Alan was surprised. Mother wouldn't sew on a button for them now. His socks were a disgrace and Madge's vest were in ribbons. He still had the

155

same pair of pyjamas that he'd worn under the dining room table during the war.

"She wanted a sewing machine, but that blasted old skinflint wouldn't buy her one . . . He said he couldn't interfere. I couldn't buy one . . . How could I?" He was appealing, the way he held his hands out to Alan. He was like Mr. Sorsky, the tailor. There was something mushy at the centre of him—over-ripe and indulgent. "I couldn't even buy her a decent pair of scissors. You don't know what it was like."

It was worse than the bad tempers, the jubilant rages, this pathetic voice murmuring on about the past. Janet would be wondering where he was. He'd promised to meet her by nine o'clock.

"Look Dad," he said. "I'm late. Will you be all right now?"

He looked at his father and away again. Father seemed to have shrunk in the battered chair. Alan couldn't be sure it wasn't an act, those fluttering eyelids, the voice thick with self-pity.

"She's a wicked woman," pronounced Father. "Rotten through and through. Comes of bad stock. She only cares about money. She'd see me begging in the street and not lift her little finger."

"Shut up, Joe," he shouted. "It's none of my business. She's just gone for a walk and I don't blame her. There's precious little to keep her here." He went into the scullery to wash his hands and face.

"She left you," Father said. "She left you with your Auntie and went off to her Father. What sort of a woman would do a thing like that?"

"I'm not listening," he cried, rubbing the roller towel hard against his face. He was turning into stone inside.

"She's been carrying on with that Sydney for weeks. Meeting him at the station. I'll turn her out . . . You see if I don't." Father was sitting upright, warming his hands at the fire. Resolve was making him stronger. "See if I care . . . You can all go hang."

"You're talking rubbish," said Alan. "You'll bring on your indigestion."

"Indigestion?" His father took the prescription out of his pocket and waved it in the air. "Indigestion? Do you know what these are for? Pills to keep me calm. I'm ill. I'm too agitated." He threw the paper on to the flames and watched it burn. "I'm damned if I'll be calm," he said.

"I won't be late," said Alan.

He hovered in the doorway, waiting for the scrap of paper to disintegate. He didn't want to meet Janet any more but he couldn't possibly stay in the house. If only they'd buy more chairs, he thought foolishly. Father bent forward as though to snatch the prescription from the fire. He stood up, butting his head against the mantelshelf. He groaned and buckled at the knees.

"Are you all right?" asked Alan, not moving.

"I'm fine," Father moaned. "It does me the world of good, dashing me brains out once a week." He pushed past Alan and began to take the bread out of the bin on the draining board. He'd eaten a big meal before he went to the doctors, but he was still peckish. "Clear off," he said, waving the carving knife at Alan. He attacked the loaf of bread as if it was a side of beef, hacking a slice as thick as a book and showering crumbs upon the mat.

When Alan was on the path, Father darted after him and caught hold of his arm; he still held the knife. "I love her," he cried. "God help me, I love her."

So that's what it's called, thought Alan, backing away and taking his bicycle from the fence. Father and Madge were very free with the word. He shivered with disgust. He knew his mother wasn't meeting another man; she'd been cured of all that living with Father.

All the same he did go and meet Janet at the club. He played ping-pong and enjoyed himself. He put his name down for a visit to the theatre in Southport. He needn't ask anyone any more; Mother had said he was adult. Janet would pay the cost of the ticket. He found it quite easy to forget what had happened earlier in the evening.

*   *   *

You could tell that Mother was disappointed by the appearance of the common room. She found it a little shabby—the worn armchairs pushed to the wall, the scraps of paper pinned to the notice board. She wouldn't admit it but she thought it was a disgrace—the fees they paid, and there wasn't even a carpet on the floor.

The boys were subdued in their best clothes; they stood self-consciously with their parents, nodding at each other, but not speaking. Some of the prefects, turned eighteen and more sophisticated, carried trays with glasses of sherry. The mothers and fathers helped themselves with effusive cries of delight—"How kind" . . . "My word, that's nice." They stood half-turned to the oak-panelled doors, waiting for the headmaster to join them. A few of the masters, dressed in dusty gowns, were already seated at small tables. They made little corrections in the margins of exercise books.

"It's a big room," said Father, looking at the broad windowsills cluttered with books, and the paint peeling from the ceiling.

"Big," agreed Mother, "but a shade scruffy for my taste." She would have had a field day with her paint brush. In her school on the continent there had been bowls of flowers and pictures of saints on the smooth immaculate walls.

There was a murmur of anticipation as the headmaster entered. He was tall and handsome with wavy hair and a firm chin. He paused to chat with parents near the door; he waved his hand to a group at the fire. Mother wore an arch, fixed smile. The headmaster crossed the room and hesitated under her stare. He said good evening and walked on. He didn't remember her, but nobody would know. She gave a little gulp of pleasure and clutched Alan's arm.

"Which is his wife, dear?"

Alan writhed under the endearment. "Over there," he muttered. "In the green frock."

"What's that?" said Father. "What's going on," and he and Mother looked in the direction of the headmaster's wife, watching her intently as she moved between the cluster of parents by the window.

The headmaster announced that he was delighted to see them all. It was to be very informal, no starchiness . . . He and the masters were here to give what help they could. As if to emphasize the point he stood in the center of the room on a level with them, pivoting round and round so that he could look everyone in the eye, his gown trailing the floor. In these changing times, the old standards swept away by the war, a young man's education was more important than ever. A good school should instill character as well as learning. The masters were here to discuss both aspects of their pupils' progress. Informally, without reserve. Unfortunately there would have to be a certain amount of queuing at each table to see the boy's individual masters . . . It couldn't be avoided and he felt sure they were all used to queues by now. The parents laughed; he was very charming. No side to him at all. At nine o'clock there would be coffee and biscuits.

"Come on," said Father. "Don't hang about." And he rushed forward to the table nearest the fire.

"That's for the upper sixth," said Alan. "You want Mr. Tomkins over there."

160

Mother stood with a sherry glass in her hand, looking round hungrily. She wanted to be spoken to, to be acknowledged. She loosened the silver fox about her shoulders and caught back the veil of her hat; the sequins glittered like snowflakes in her hair.

"Where do we go?" she called in a shrill affected voice. "Do pause for little me."

Alan waited by the door with several of his class mates. Like him, they were ashamed to be seen with their parents.

"Look at Lacey's dad," murmured someone. "He's overdone the sherry." They were all relieved at the sight of Lacey senior standing unsteadily in front of the fire.

Now that it was actually happening, the occasion he had dreaded, Alan felt better. It was out of his hands. In an hour or two his parents would know the worst. On the journey home there would be recriminations. Further time would pass with Father standing on the porch looking out for Madge. The following day they would nag him cruelly, a little less the day after—in a week it would be back to normal. Normal for them. He stood in his new suit with the waistcoat to match, and eased his starched collar away from his neck. To survive he had learned not to show his feelings. When he'd been younger, he was always losing things—toys, articles of clothing. When he was shouted at he stood very still and kept his face blank. He never batted an eyelid. Confronted with such indifference, they left him alone. In the car it would be dark. He could shut his eyes and let them rant.

At coffee-and-biscuits time, Mother and Father were to be seen with his housemaster. They didn't seem upset. Father was holding Mr. Rufus by the arm and talking into his ear. After a moment Mr. Rufus broke into a loud guffaw of laughter. Mother nodded at Alan, but absentmindedly—his might have been a face she'd glimpsed from a train; she was absorbed in conversation with the headmaster's wife. The four of them were bobbing about in the center of the room, touching each other's arm and smiling. The headmaster joined them—the group scattered out of deference, then reformed and closed ranks tighter than before. From his position at the door, Alan thought they resembled a troop of Morris dancers, with Mother as the maypole. Other parents, not in the golden circle, hovered enviously at their heels. Alan was astonished. Over the years his mother and father had attended the school irregularly. He was a scholarship boy. They didn't come to Sports Days. He couldn't think what they were doing to make themselves so popular.

"Is that your mother?" Lacey asked him. He pretended he hadn't heard. The headmaster had taken Mother by the elbow; the silver fox trembled about her face. Shrill and clear like a trumpet call came his mother's flamboyant laugh.

After some minutes, regretfully the headmaster moved on and gave his attention to the waiting parents. Exhausted, Mother flopped into a chair and fanned herself with her glove. She sat with her knees spread wide apart as if she was by the fire at home.

Father beckoned Alan, but he looked the other way. He went out of the door and stood in the deserted corridor. Father followed him and took his arm; they strolled slowly towards the science laboratory. "I don't mind telling you," Father said. "We're a little taken aback by what we've heard. Yes, indeed."

"What have you heard?"

"You've been slacking," said Father. "That's obvious. You'll need extra tutoring in Latin. I'll have a word with Mr. Harrison."

"I'm off Latin," he said.

"As Mother's explained it, you don't have much option. You need Latin for the law."

They passed the door of the gymnasium, turned and retraced their steps. In the distance ragged, like music played out of doors, came the strains of the school orchestra practicing in the assembly hall.

Father stopped and listened. "Why didn't you do something with the piano," he said irritably. "All those lessons you've had. I've only heard you play one blithering tune."

"They don't have much call for pianos," he said. "It's mostly violins and cellos."

"Well, you should have played some of those. When I think of—" He pulled himself together and walked on.

"Did they say I'd get a bad report?" asked Alan.

"No," said Father, "they didn't." He drew out

his handkerchief and blew his nose. He looked as
if he wanted to say something important. Instead
he said emotionally: "You stop worrying, son. You
take things too seriously."

Father was trying to be kind; it couldn't have
been easy for him, struggling as he was to forget
the price of Mrs. Evan's music lessons. It was puz-
zling. If he wasn't due for a bad report, what on
earth was wrong?

In the car going home Mother and Father
were both elated. What an enjoyable evening—
how charming the headmaster had been! What
was that rubbish Alan had told them about Mr.
Rufus being a dried-up old stick?

"Isn't it odd?" observed Mother. "That
woman had no dress sense whatever. You'd think
she'd know what's what."

"She had a nice way with her, though," said
Father. "She wasn't in the least stuck up."

"What did Mr. Tomkins have to say?" asked
Alan.

"You have a lot of ability," said Mother. "A lot
of ability. Of course you don't stretch yourself. You
go to that club too much. You shouldn't read so
many comics."

"I don't read any," he protested.

Her voice became shriller. "You don't put
yourself out."

"Ease up," said Father. "Abide by their ad-
vice, Connie. They're educated men."

"If there's one thing I can't stand," she said,
"it's laziness."

"Hush up," advised Father. He squirmed on his seat and tried to find Alan's face in the driving mirror. It was too dark. Mother leaned her head against the seat and dozed.

The car sped past the disused lighthouse and the estuary; the headlamps flashed across the heaped sand blown against the boathouse door.

"You're a touch secretive," said Father. "I understand it, mind you. When I was a lad I kept back one or two things from your Aunt Nora. Nothing too big, mind. Climbing roofs, that sort of thing. The young have a right to their secrets." He sounded pompous. He was a liar; if he'd thought Alan was keeping a secret, he would have wrung his neck to learn it.

In the darkness, a mile away, Madge was cavorting with her unknown German.

· 7 ·

THEY were all going down to the shore for an airing. It was one of Mother's impulses. Janet Leyland had telephoned Alan in the morning and Mother answered; she invited Janet for Saturday tea.

"It's a beautiful day," she said. "We could all go for a little walk." She put the phone down. Seeing Alan standing in the hall, she scolded: "Take your shoes off. She's coming to tea." It might have been her friend and nothing to do with him.

Father was summoned from the greenhouse and told of the outing.

"Are we going in the car?" he asked.

"No," Mother said. "It's a beautiful day. It's fresh air you need."

"Is that so?" he said testily. "I suppose it's stale air in our back garden."

167

All the same, he went upstairs to change his clothes. Mother wore her spring coat and a head-scarf and her white courtshoes. She carried a hand-bag. She took Father's arm at first, leaving Alan and Janet to walk behind, but she was moved by a show of daffodils in the garden of the bungalow next door to the farm. She stepped backwards, neatly severing the two of them asunder and clung to Janet's arm, pointing at the yellow flowers stiffly bordering the patch of lawn.

"Look at them," she cried. "Oooh, look at that hydrangea." Haltingly they proceeded down the lane towards the railway crossing. "Winter's dying," she proclaimed, tilting her bright face to the sky and stumbling in her high-heeled shoes.

Father marched self-consciously ahead, military fashion, with swinging arms. He wasn't used to walks. Though he'd changed into a sports jacket, he still wore his beret. Mother and Janet followed, clutching their handbags and bouncing chummily against each other. In the rear walked Alan.

The season was changing; the branches of the trees were beginning to thicken with tight black buds; on the waste ground besides the goods-yard the forsythia bush had burst into bloom. Even so, as they crossed the railway line, a chill little breeze tore down the cinder track and whirled the dust into their faces. In slow procession they sauntered awkwardly down the road.

"We had a garden with a swing," Mother was saying. "And one of those double seats under a striped awning. My Father gave it to me."

"It was broken," said Father, eavesdropping.

"And a wrought-iron table, painted white."

"I like white," said Janet.

They passed the wool shop and the grocers and the last gray-stone house, set in a wilderness of uncut grass and black-currant bushes. It had been taken over by evacuees during the war; the seesaw still lay in the grass—a barrel and a plank of wood —rotting beneath a chestnut tree. Straight between the flat fields hedged with hawthorn ran the dirt lane to the sea. On one side there was a ditch clogged with reeds, upon whose banks two boys sat hopefully, dangling jam jars on lengths of string.

"It's very bracing," said Mother, headscarf fluttering.

"It's blasted freezing," Father said.

The sun stripped the fields of color; under the white and glittering sky only the distant pines showed dark blue against the horizon. Buffeted by the wind, the family walked in single file through the bleached landscape.

When the path cut through the woods, they were more sheltered. Amidst trees opposite the vicarage, stood a wooden shack with a solitary bell hanging in the porch. Alan and Madge had attended Sunday school there. Madge used to pile the crimson hassocks one on top of the other and kneel high and eager above the pews. When she overbalanced and sprawled upon the floor she pretended to be dead. They were given pictures with sticky backs to paste in books—St. John the Baptist, the baby Jesus crowned with golden curls, Elijah and the ravens. Madge called Jesus "Bubbles." In summer the door of the shack was left open. The sand seeped over the top step of the dark hut. Along the path to the railway crossing, Madge leapt backwards and forwards across the ditch. She came home with her socks mucky.

"Look at that," shouted Father. He had snapped a stick from an alder bush and was pointing nostalgically at the shack. "Remember that, son?"

"What about it?" muttered Alan. Did Father think he was suffering from amnesia? Sunday school was only yesterday.

Disappointed, Father strode on, swiping at the air with his stick.

There were a few cars parked on the sandy verge beside the wire netting. The army had put up the fencing because of the unexploded shells.

"God knows where they get the petrol," said Father, scowling at drivers dozing over the wheel. He bought his on the black market.

Alan wished his Mother would stop looking at people as they passed. She had a curiously intense stare, like a greedy child waiting for sweets. Someone waved to him from the window of a car. It was Hilda Fennel, out for a spin with her parents. He nodded his head in recognition.

"Someone you know?" asked Mother, turning round to have a good look.

He denied it.

"But you nodded. I saw you."

"Something got stuck in my eye," he said.

"Who was it, pet?" asked Janet.

He wouldn't answer. She shouldn't have been taken over; it was Madge's place to be hanging on Mother's arm.

The sunlight was bewildering after the months of gray days. It shone on the chrome bumpers of the cars, on the pale leaves of the eucalyptus bushes. The slender saplings of birch that grew in the hollow beneath the ridge of pines fluttered silver in the breeze.

"Isn't it just beautiful," cried Mother, shading her eyes, dazzled by the shimmering light.

Father was determined to walk further. He led them beyond the woods until the path narrowed between stretches of gorse and dune. The marram grasses that bound the sand to the earth flickered like strips of metal in the sunlight. The last telegraph pole was reached; the cinder path petered out. Ahead lay the sea, far out across the brown waste of shore. The beach was strewn with driftwood, whorled, salt-encrusted, piled in heaps by the tide. Everywhere they looked was wreckage—pieces of timber, empty crates, the smashed hulks of small fishing boats. The margin of the sea was flecked with ring-plover and oyster catchers. When the waves broke the birds rose in the air and wheeled inland.

"What a mess," cried Father, trousers flapping, hands anchoring the beret to his head.

Now they were here, there wasn't anything particular for them to do. Mother turned her back on the sea. She and Janet jigged up and down on the spot to keep warm. Across the ridges of crushed shells and tumbled sand lay the brown streamers of kelp, bulbs swollen, stinking of iodine.

"What a mess," repeated Father, staring bleakly about him; what a time he could have with his carpet sweeper.

"You two go off on your own," ordered Mother, relinquishing her hold on Janet. She tottered toward Father and sheltered behind his back.

Alan walked away down the beach. The wind swelled his clothes and bore him along. He heard Janet calling him. Ignoring her, he began to climb the cliffs of sand, gripping the tufts of marram to pull himself higher. He intended to get right away from her, but half way up the rise the grass cut the palm of his hand. He faced the sea and sat down, licking the beads of blood and tasting salt on his tongue. He waited for Janet to catch up with him. She came nearer, her face obscured by the thin silk of her billowing headscarf. Climbing laboriously up the dune she flopped down beside him. She couldn't speak; her breath had given out. Down on the shore his parents huddled together, small and black, like a bundle of blown rags. Janet stole a glance at him—he knew that look of hers. She saw him as a dear little boy whom nobody understood.

He showed her his hand.

"You poor little lad," she murmured, dragging the scarf from her hair and tying it about his palm.

"Get off," he said. "It's nothing."

But he was pleased she took care of it. That's

what women were for—to be practical and sympathetic. They weren't much good for anything else.

"Don't be cross," she said. "Just because I was nice to your Mum. I'd much rather have walked with you."

"I don't mind either way," he said.

"She's got such nice ways . . . She makes you feel—" She couldn't think of the exact word she wanted.

"Nice," he said, teasing her.

She turned her head away in annoyance. The frizzed ends of her hair shook in the wind. "She's nicer than you at any rate," she snapped. "She communicates. She said she went to a finishing school."

"She did," he said. "With nuns."

"She's never a Catholic?"

"No, but she went to a convent."

"She speaks French," said Janet with wonder. "She can play the piano."

She irritated him, going on about his mother's accomplishments, screaming her praises above the howling of the wind. What had it got to do with her where his mother went to school? The sight of her, flesh impregnable under the armour of that enormous coat, stout legs encased in winter boots, filled him with fury. Spitefully he pushed her sideways so that she lost her balance. She brought her gloved hand up to brush the hair from her face. Sand flew into her eye. She sat crouched over, blinking, whining like a child. He had no patience with her. He scrambled on all fours up the slope, kicking sand behind him like a dog digging a hole. At the very top he straightened and ran headlong down the other side. He was in a shallow valley set among the undulating dunes, earthed with low bushes and clumps of gorse, protected from the wind. He lay on his stomach and rested his head on his arms. He fretted that he couldn't lie there for long, but had to worry about his Mother and Father shivering on the beach and Janet whining behind the sand hill. If he were more like Madge, he'd be able to do as he wanted . . . It was then he heard his sister's voice. He thought for a moment he'd conjured it up in his head. He stopped breathing. A man spoke. Madge said something else, but he couldn't make out the sense of it. He looked up and stared about him. He couldn't see anyone. The man began to sing in a language he didn't understand.

"Stop," he heard Madge say. "Sing it slower."

The voice began again, exaggeratedly dragging out the words as if it was a record on a gramophone that had begun to wind down. He didn't know why he felt so angry—the foolishness of her: in broad daylight, with his parents strolling the sands. He inched forward on his belly; he made such a noise he thought Madge was bound to rise from cover like a startled bird. They were somewhere to his left beyond the gorse bushes, behind a small hillock. He didn't know what he was going to do when he caught them. The scarf shook free from his hand and bowled away in the breeze; he hardly noticed. It was like him and Ronnie Baines playing at commandoes when they were boys. Slithering up the dune he peered cautiously down. Madge was lying flat on her back with her panama hat tipped over her eyes. She had her arms spread wide on the soft bed of drifted sand. The prisoner in his green uniform, a black diamond of cloth sewn to the back of his tunic, lay half on top of her. He had brown shoes and white socks. Madge's school blouse was unbuttoned to the waist. Her raincoat was bunched up. The man was nuzzling her breast and mournfully singing. Even as Alan watched, she brought up her hand, in a gesture he recognized as infinitely tender, began to stroke the man's head.

Alan almost sniggered aloud. He fell backwards, careless of the noise he made, and rolled down the slope. Picking himself up he leapt over the stretches of gorse towards the dunes. Janet was still sat hunched in the sand, shielding her face. He dragged her to her feet and tugged her down the cliff.

"Stop it," she complained.

She tried to pull her hand away but he wouldn't let go. They lunged down the hill and dropped the few remaining feet on to the beach. He was laughing.

"What's so funny?" she asked crossly, struggling upright and attempting to brush the wet sand from her clothes. There was an anklet of seaweed clinging to her boot. He rocked backwards and forwards on his haunches with his mouth wide open. He had a piece of gorse stuck to his pullover, coiling outwards like a strand of wire.

"Whatever's the matter," she said. "Look at the state of you."

"I saw Madge," he said. "With a bloke . . . back there." He waved his hand in the direction of the cliff.

"Where's my headscarf," she wanted to know.

He sat on the beach, silent now, his face white and grains of sand like stubble grazing his cheek. He was thinking of Madge in her old panama in all that waste of land. She hadn't been wearing a liberty bodice—she didn't seem to feel the cold. Why didn't she act shy—they'd both had the same up-bringing? The image of her, those white fingers threading the man's hair, the white skin of her body tinged with blue by the shadow of her open blouse, filled him with regret. He felt forlorn, cheated—why couldn't things be like that for him? He shivered and covered his face with his arm.

"What were they doing?" Janet asked. She sounded belligerent.

"Singing," he said.

"Singing?"

She dragged his arm away. Her nose was red. One eye was inflamed from rubbing at it, and there was a crust of dried sand at the corner of her mouth. He couldn't imagine her undoing one button of that blasted coat without the blood freezing in her veins.

"Why are you so upset?" she demanded, still in that harsh, matter-of-fact voice.

She looked down the beach to see if his parents were in sight. The shore was deserted. The tide was coming in, the sky darkening. That much nearer, on delicate legs, the seabirds stalked the edge of the waves.

"You didn't see them," he said. "They're not like you and me."

She knew he was criticizing her. "What's that supposed to mean," she asked. "What are we like, then?"

"We're not like anything," he said. "That's what we're like."

"Just because we don't go about singing," she retorted. She was near to tears herself. She left him. She plodded off down the beach. Only a short way. She returned and stood looking down at him, all her curls messed up and her lipstick smeared. "I don't understand you," she said dully, unable to touch him. "I'm out of my depth."

*   *   *

His school was one stop down the line from Madge's. He said he had a dental appointment and he left early and got out at Crosby and waited outside the station for her. Madge was late. Other girls came in their school uniforms and ran down the ramp towards the barrier. He turned the corner thinking he might have missed her. She was standing alone with an umbrella in her hand, facing a line of grammar-school boys, taunting them. She was in her ankle socks in a puddle of rainwater with her shoes tied to her satchel by the laces. He dodged out of sight. He heard shouts and running feet. The boys ran out into the main road and Madge followed brandishing her umbrella. A boy in short trousers, cap rammed sideways over his ear, stopped to face her. He swung his bulky brief-case in an arc and caught Madge on the side of the head. She sprang forward and whacked him on the shoulder. He ran, red in the face, after his friends.

She saw him standing against the wall. "Hallo, Alan," she said. "Fancy seeing you."

"You must be mad," he said. "What do you want to behave like that for?"

"A bit of combat," she said, "does one the world of good." She was trying to kiss his cheek—in the road, with all the people passing by.

Madge wouldn't go down the ramp like any normal person. She insisted on dragging him through a gap in the hoardings behind the station. He tore his coat on a nail. She was through in a flash, seating herself upon the wooden seat on the platform. The train had gone.

"I saw you," he said. "On Saturday." He had to say it quickly otherwise his annoyance at finding her brawling in the street might have sidetracked him.

"Saturday?" she said, wide-eyed.

"It's no use," he said. "I saw you in the sand with that German."

"Oh," she said.

"I'm worried stiff."

"You're very naughty," she chided. "It's rude to spy on people."

178

"Don't," he pleaded.

On the opposite platform the grammar-school boys had appeared. They shouted insults across the track.

"Run along," she called. "Don't be silly little boys."

"Madge," he said. "You're too young. It's not right to go with men of that age."

"There's no rules," she said. "You can't lay down rules." She was pulling faces at the boys scuffling and parading for her benefit on the far platform. "The trouble with you is you're too hidebound."

"Put your shoes on," he said.

"You're old before your time. In years to come, lads like you will take to drink, or aspirins. Mark my words."

He would have liked to bash her. Instead he said: "It's Mum and Dad I'm thinking of. All they've taught you—"

"I was taught nothing," she snapped. "By anyone. Mother said I'd cut myself when I had me first period."

"Don't," he moaned. "People will hear."

"You don't have to worry," she told him. She was looking at him tenderly as if he was the one who needed forgiving. "I love him. He was captured in Russia. He walked across the frozen snow."

He had a picture in his head of Mr. Sorsky, with his tapemeasure trailing across the ice. "It's not relevant," he said.

"Then he went to America. He wasn't old. He

was stuck behind barbed wire. Think of it . . . looking at black women swollen with disease."

"Leprosy?" he queried. "That's Africa."

She took no notice. She said the stares of the negro women had been a torment.

He couldn't think what she meant—those dusky maidens with unmentionable medical histories swaying melon-hipped beyond the compound. "What was he doing in America?" he asked, dumbfounded.

"He's going away—"

"Good thing," he said. "When I saw you—"

"Don't tell me you and Janet thingy don't touch each other."

"We don't," he cried, stung by the truth of it.

The train came in on the other side. The boys crowded the windows of the compartment and flattened their noses against the glass. Madge waved her umbrella in farewell.

"He's going away," she repeated dismally. "He's being repatriated. Any moment. I want to go with him." She didn't look desperately unhappy. Her voice was quite bouncy and confident. "Before the war," she said, "he worked in a garage. He's got a motorbike. He thinks the Russians might have taken it. He's got a sister." She nudged his arm as if to accentuate how alike they were, he and the prisoner of war.

"You'd undone your clothes," he said. His cheeks flamed.

"I didn't. He did."

"You both need horsewhipping."

"You're like Dad," she said. "You think everything's rude."

"It's wrong." He thumped the seat to emphasise his point of view.

"You know," she said, looking down at her stockinged feet rimmed with mud. "It's no wonder I don't wear shoes. Never being able to wear them in the house."

"There's other things you're not supposed to do," he cried. "You don't worry about that."

"When he goes," she said. "I'll kill myself. I can't live without him."

A girl came along the platform and passed them on the bench. She called "hallo" to Madge.

"That's Betty Foster," Madge told him. "Don't you think she's got big bosoms."

"When's he going?" asked Alan.

"Soon," she said. She bit her fingernail and looked gloomily along the track. "He's so beautiful. Did you think he looked beautiful?"

"I didn't see his face. I saw your hat."

"We were only getting close," she said. "We didn't do anything. But I might before he goes. I'd like him to be the first."

There was no way he could make her see sense. Maybe she knew more than he did. "Think of Mother," he said.

"It's got nothing to do with Mum. She's made her mistakes. They've got you on their conscience."

"Me," he said, flabbergasted.

"All the stuff the teachers told them at your school meeting."

"What stuff—"

"You're nervy . . . highly strung . . . They told Father you might have a breakdown."

"Rubbish," he shouted.

The girl Madge knew, loitering at the end of the platform, turned to look.

"You take things too seriously. Walking round the village with that Janet . . . looking hunted. Bothering about Dad and his indigestion. Worrying yourself sick about Mum going out. You're persecuted."

"They can't have said that," he protested. "You're making it up."

The train was approaching.

"Some of it," Madge admitted. "But not all."

She advanced down the platform, swinging her umbrella like Charlie Chaplin. She spoke to the girl with the large measurements.

He wouldn't travel with them. He got into a first class compartment and spent the journey standing like a hunchback, with his satchel on his shoulders.

*   *   *

Even Mother was turning against Madge. There was something sinister in the way the girl stayed out late night after night and didn't seem to care about the displeasure she incurred. It was

182

harmless, of course, going out walking, even if it was in the dark, but what if she took a step forward and decided to take up smoking or give up school? She looked exhausted in the mornings; she could hardly drag herself out of bed. If she'd have whined when rebuked, or answered insolently, it would have been easier to cope with; but she was so reasonable, so patient.

"I do no harm," she said. "You're wrong. I'm right."

"It's not normal," Mother told Alan.

"I warned you," he said. "You wouldn't listen." He thought if they could just hang on for a little longer, until the prisoner was sent back to Germany, it would be all right. If he told the truth heavens knows what trouble would be caused. Mother and Father wouldn't deal with it themselves—they'd call in the vicar and the headmistress of the school. Obviously if the German was staying it would be different. Then he'd have to tell them. So he kidded himself.

He apologized to Janet Leyland for pushing her down in the sand. He tried to go into details about Madge and the prisoner, but for some reason she didn't want to know. She'd stopped being interested in his family. She didn't telephone him after school. When he called at her house on Wednesday night, her mother said she had gone to the cinema with Moira. He thought Mrs. Leyland wasn't as pleased to see him as usual. She didn't ask him in. Immediately he began to wonder if Janet no longer cared for him. He told himself she was

bound to ring him as soon as she came back. He
waited at home for three hours—in the hall—in
case the wireless drowned the ringing of the bell.
He felt wretched. The next day it was worse; it was
as if he'd grown used to sitting in a warm room,
everybody noticing him, and suddenly the door
had been kicked in his face, leaving him outside.
He couldn't sit still. He avoided Ronnie on the
train. He was always imagining she would be waiting for him round the next corner, the next hedge,
beside the gates of the park. He didn't go to the
club; he was afraid she would snub him openly.

He sat in the kitchen with Father, listening to
snatches of poetry and string quartets.

"Thrown you out of the club, have they?"
asked Father. He preferred to sit either with
Madge or on his own. Alan was too restless.

"I've some homework," Alan said.

"Well, get in the front room and stop messing
about."

Alan laid the ironing cloth on the table and
opened his books.

Mother came downstairs. She poked her head
round the door and said: "Mind the table."

She went out and slammed the front door.
Father was through in an instant.

"That damned woman," he wailed. "She's left
me again."

"She's going to flower-arranging classes," said
Alan, inspired.

"In winter?" said Father. "What blasted flowers?"

"There's something different each night," Alan said. "It's not just flowers." He couldn't think what Mother was up to. If she had been off to meet Captain Sydney, she'd have gone decked out like a flower herself. She'd have worn her furs and her paste jewelry, not her old coat and headscarf.

"I'll teach her," cried Father. "I'll show her what's what." He prowled round the cold room in his slippers. They were made of red canvas.

"Did you get those off Madge?" Alan asked, unable to take his eyes from Father's poppy-coloured feet prancing over the carpet.

"If she's not home by ten o'clock," Father said, "I'll break her neck . . . You see if I don't." He went back into the kitchen, slamming the door with such force the clock chimed the hour. It was only a quarter to eight.

Perhaps Mother had slipped next door to visit Mrs. Frobisher. It wasn't likely—she thought her common. Maybe she'd gone to the pictures. He couldn't concentrate on his books. Everytime he looked at the illustrations in his history book he saw Janet's face. He found himself writing her name in the margin of his exercise book, over and over. He thought if ever she forgave him and he got the chance he'd quite suddenly go off with another girl. Her friend Moira, for one. It would serve her right. He lay with his head on one bent arm for what seemed a long time, staring down at the table. It must be getting late. He tiptoed into the hall and looked at the grandfather clock. It was twenty minutes to ten. Mother wouldn't come in for another hour, he was sure. Carefully he opened the glass case of the clock and moved the hands back to just under the quarter. He did it very abruptly so as to stop the half hour from chiming. He'd sat down at the table before he remembered the clock in the lounge. The wireless was loud in the kitchen; it made it easier to enter the back room without Father hearing. The clock was on the mantelpiece, set between the boy with the violin and the lady sitting on a lump of rock. He had to alter it in the dark, prising the circular disc off the back and being careful not to trap his fingers on the key. It had a cruel mechanism. Mother had tried to teach Madge the time by it when she was five years old—she made Madge reset it every time she got the hour wrong—the ends of her small fingers bled. Father wound pieces of cotton wool round them and Mother cried tears of remorse. Even now Madge said time didn't count, it was man-made; she refused to recognize it.

When he replaced the clock on the mantelpiece he couldn't hear it ticking. He shook it but nothing happened.

"Alan," called Father, from behind the wall. "What are you up to?"

"I'm looking for the dictionary," he said. He closed the door guiltily behind him.

When Madge came in he called out to her when she hung her coat in the hall.

"What do you want?" she said. "Hurry up, I've got to humor Dad."

"Mum's gone missing again."

"So what?" she said. She looked as if she'd been squeezed to death under a sandbag. The brim of her panama hat was unravelling. She went in to Father and kicked the kitchen door shut.

Later she brought a cup of tea through to him. She placed it in the empty grate so as not to harm the table.

"He's all right now," she said. "I've jollied him up."

"What's come over her?" he asked. "Where does she go all the time?"

"He's like a spoilt child," said Madge. "He's got no sense of discipline."

"He has cause," he said hotly. "She's always out."

"Where's your Janet thingy then? Has she chucked you?"

"It was your fault," he told her. "She was with me when I saw you with that Jerry."

"That's right," Madge said. "Blame somebody else. You and my Dad . . . My hat, you're a pair." And she looked at him as if he crawled out from under a stone.

He collected his books together and wiped the table with his sleeve.

She said: "He's going on Sunday."

"Good riddance."

"He wants me to have the seventh heaven—"

He looked at her astounded. "The what?"

"You know . . . It . . . I'm going to do it."

"It?"

"Everything," she said. "Whatever he wants. So he'll have something to remember me by."

"You blasted fool," he cried. "You'll land yourself in trouble. You'll have something to remember all right."

"I know," she said gloomily. "But I promised."

"If you had a decent mother," he shouted in fury, "if she wasn't off gallivanting with that friend of Mr. Harrison's, she might have time to notice what you're up to." He regretted he altered the clocks. He wished she'd come home quick so that Father could break her neck.

"Gallivanting?" Madge said. "Mother? You daft fool. She's in the waiting room at the station. She sits by the fire with her library book."

Oh God, he thought, it's true . . . There's no one telling her she looks nice. "The neighbors," he said. "What if she's seen?" He sat down at the table and turned his back on Madge.

"Haven't you learnt," she said, "that it's never important to anyone else. Not really. It's a nine days' wonder. You're only inconvenienced. You're not upset inside." And she had the audacity to put her arm round his neck and beat upon his breast with her clenched fist. He flung her off.

Hearing the commotion Father came into the front room and demanded an explanation.

"He's feeling sensitive," Madge told him. "He's had a tiff with his girlfriend."

Father said they were a couple of savages. "Do you want everyone to know our business?" he whispered, gesturing frantically at the party wall.

Madge laughed loudly. She went up the stairs sniggering. Father ran after her into the hall, shouting he didn't know how he'd come by such blasted offspring.

"You can say that again," Madge cried. It made her laugh more than ever.

In the night a storm blew up. The branches of the sycamore tree thrashed against the windows of the upstairs room. Shortly before dawn the pane of glass nearest the chest of drawers shattered and fell into the porch.

· 8 ·

ON FRIDAY night Madge stayed in. She confided to Alan that her German had gone into the village to say goodbye to the vicar and his wife. It was just as well because she wanted to keep an eye on Father. He'd come home early and spent two hours making a botched-up job of putting a piece of wood in Mother's window. He couldn't seem to cut it to the right size. When he'd finished he had to screw up newspapers and stuff them down the sides. Mother said it looked ridiculous. He was threatening yet again to chop down the sycamore tree. "The blasted thing's a menace. Choking the drains . . . smashing the glass."

"The frame was rotten," argued Madge. "It wasn't the willow tree's fault."

Alan asked Mother if he could light a fire in the back room. He knew he was wasting his breath

—it was cheaper for Mother to sit at the station.

"You keep out of my room," she said. "Somebody's been fiddling with my clock." She was in the lounge for quite ten minutes trying to get it to work. "Alan," she shouted. "It's broken." She came into the hall and waved it in his face.

"Oh heck," he said awkwardly. "Perhaps you've overwound it."

"Me?" she said. "Me?" She was crying in the worst way, silently, without moving her mouth; the tears dripped down her cheeks. They both stood in the doorway of the lounge and watched her replace the clock on the mantelpiece. She was wearing a pair of Father's old socks and Madge's army slippers. She stroked the glass case and bowed her head.

"It'll mend," said Madge.

"Go away," Mother said. "Let me be"—as though she needed to be left alone with the dead.

They heard her go upstairs and after a while, when she had rinsed her face, come down. Alan and Madge began to talk in loud voices to cover the sound of her leaving the house. Father heard all the same. He huddled in his chair reading the newspaper, one thumb bound with sticking plaster from his carpentry on the upstairs window. He had decided there was nothing worth listening to on the wireless. The room was perfectly quiet save for the scrape of Madge's pencil as she drew at the table. It seemed to Alan, sitting there with nothing to do, that the silence extended far beyond the confines of the house, encompassing his empty school, the church, the streets, the waiting room where his mother sat in spectacles, reading her stories of mystery and romance. It will go on for ever, he thought, looking about the room, at the single light bulb dangling from the ceiling, last summer's flypaper, the spread of newsprint behind which his father crouched. Who would prevent the whole of his existence from continuing in this silent fashion? For the rest of his life, until he was an old man, he felt he would hear the absence of the ticking clock in the lounge, the stillness of his mother's vacant bedroom.

There was a knock at the front door. Father threw down his newspaper and scuttled in scarlet slippers to the scullery.

"If it's Mr. Harrison," he whispered. "Tell him I'm not here. I'm not in the mood for visitors."

He locked the back door as a precaution, as if he expected his friend to barge up the side path and force an entry. Even in all this activity and bustle—the falling paper, the lock turning like a pistol shot—the house remained silent as the grave.

"The bathroom window's not shut," Madge said. "You want to be careful he doesn't shin up the drain pipe."

Alan opened the door. The sight of Janet Leyland, standing on the porch in her woolly hat, made him tremble. He hadn't lost her after all. But almost as soon as she had entered the hall and he saw her clearly, warm coat belted, sensible boots planted upon the crimson carpeting, he wondered what it was he had been frightened of losing.

"It's you," he said.

"I've just seen your mother. She said it was all right to call."

"She had to go out," he explained.

"She said we should go upstairs to your room, so as not to disturb your Dad."

"I don't know about that," he said.

He looked at the door of the lounge and hesitated. He called Madge. She came bounding into the hall, demanding officiously: "What do you want? I'm a busy woman you know." She ignored Janet.

"Do you think it's all right for us to go upstairs. Mother told her we could."

"How should I know? What do you want to do?" She looked at him pityingly.

"I could call another time," Janet suggested, taking a step towards the front door.

"Come on," he said, making up his mind, and he went up the stairs ahead of her.

She thought his room was very cosy. On the furniture, transfers of rabbits and ducks showed through the white paint. "Ain't they sweet," she exclaimed, peering at the toadstools, the bunnies standing on hind legs.

"It's nursery furniture," he said. "From our old house in Hoylake." He had a wardrobe, a chest of drawers and a settle in which Mother kept the blankets.

"I called at your house," he said. The fact that he could have waited filled him with resentment.

194

"I know you did."

"You were out."

"I'm not clairvoyant," she said.

He was upsetting her all over again. She was tracing with her gloved finger the outline of ducks on the wardrobe door. Awkwardly he took a step forward and embraced her; he hadn't drawn the curtains and was worried in case Mrs. Frobisher saw them. Janet stood stiff and unresponsive, one hand resting on the wardrobe. He touched the waist of her coat and asked: "Aren't you hot?"

"It's not too warm up here," she said, as if they were in the Himalayas. She began however to undo the belt of her coat and remove her knitted gloves. "You haven't got any pictures," she observed. "Or toys."

"Toys?" he scoffed.

"Things," she said. "Model aeroplanes."

"They're under the stairs," he told her. "My trainset and Meccano. I've got things stored under the bed as well."

She was wearing a woollen dress and a cardigan; she put her handbag down on the settle and folded her arms. "Where was your mother off to this time of night? She looked very pale."

"It's the street lamps," he said. "She's gone to see a friend."

He bent her over backwards and kissed her as he'd seen them do on the films. It took a lot of stamina not to overbalance and topple to the floor; the heel of her shoe dug into his foot. He kept one eye open just in case they stumbled against the

195

chest of drawers and knocked over the vase standing on its paper doylie. One side of Janet's cardigan
hung down to the floor—he saw Madge lying in the
sand with her blouse unbuttoned. He moved so
abruptly Janet fell against the wardrobe.

"What's wrong now?" she cried, eyes sparkling, her cheeks rosy.

"Sorry," he said. "Cramp." And he rubbed his
leg. She looked better after he'd kissed her. He
couldn't take his eyes from her flushed face, her
softly swollen mouth.

"I missed you, pet," she said. "I cried every
night."

"I missed you," he mumbled.

"Madge told me to come. I met her on the
train. She said we shouldn't be silly."

"She should mind her own business."

"Is she still seeing that Jerry?"

"No," he lied. "He's been sent back home
. . . to Germany."

"Well then," she said. "That's a load off your
mind."

Madge came in with a tray of tea. She'd
remembered the sugar bowl but she hadn't pro-
vided saucers.

"Is he all right?" asked Alan. "Has he said anything."

"Nothing sensible," said Madge. She asked Janet if she wanted sugar.

Janet said Yes please and sat down on the bed.
Just in time Alan pulled her upright and carefully
drew back the counterpane and laid it neatly over
the end of the bed-post.

"You've no bedding," said Janet, looking in surprise at the lumpy ticking of the mattress.

"It's in the wash," he said. "I'm putting clean sheets on later."

"He doesn't sleep here," said Madge. "He sleeps with his Dad."

"Haven't you enough blankets?" asked Janet, after a pause.

"Plenty," said Madge. "It's other things we're short of. I've got a room too but I have to share with Mother. It's to stop them getting in the same bed. Would you like a biscuit?"

Alan stood transfixed while Madge was talking, staring at Janet Leyland wrapped in wool, perched on the extreme edge of his unused bed. Even as he watched her she brought up her hand, still clasping the handle of her cup, as though to ward off a blow. She smiled in shock. A rash of small red spots began to spread across her sensitive cheeks. At that moment he started to think of his mother, walking in an orchard . . . or was it simply the garden of the big house in Hoylake? It was a summer evening . . . She strolled with Father into the green darkness of the apple trees, humming a little song. He ran a few paces behind, watching her cling to Father's arm. It was a happy song . . . He caught up with them and pushed Father away . . . He seized his mother's hand. Father laughed and walked back alone up the garden . . .

"He keeps everything bottled up," said Madge. "Anything for a quiet life."

They were both watching him, Madge defiant, Janet with a queerly elated smile, as if she now had

197

the advantage. He wanted to make some crude joke, some inconsequential remark that wouldn't betray him.

"Take no notice of her," he said finally. "It's only temporary. The room's damp. It's just until we get the wall fixed."

"Or Father," Madge said. She began to gather the cups together. She stole a glance at him. Already she was sorry she had been so outspoken. He understood her; she came out with things for precisely the reasons he hid them—to avoid embarrassment. When the rare visitors called and Father was moody, it was Madge's way to run to the door and announce: "He's in a dreadful temper . . . I'm telling you." The guests stood shaken and alarmed, but having warned them, Madge could relax.

"I must go," Janet said. "I promised Mother I'd only pop out for an hour."

She reached for her coat. She didn't wait to put it on in the bedroom. She followed Madge hurriedly down the stairs as though she couldn't bear to be left alone with him. In the hall she leaned forward and kissed his cheek. Like a sister.

"Don't think about it, Alan," she said kindly. "All families have their problems." Possibly she was thinking of Uncle Arthur.

*　　*　　*

Saturday it was raining. The wind blew in gusts, shaking the branches of the trees and flattening

198

the privet hedge. Alan was glad. He couldn't think that Madge's Jerry would deflower her in weather like this. Before lunch, the piece of wood wedged in the upstairs window flew across the room like a bird and damaged the wallpaper. Grandfather's picture fell face down on the chest of drawers. Father wouldn't come indoors at one o'clock; Alan took his dinner on a plate to the greenhouse. He was sitting on an upturned barrel staring out at the garden. From a distance, approaching him with sausage and bacon, his face appeared to be blurred with weeping.

"Come on in," urged Alan.

"Go to hell," said Father.

He ran back up the garden, leaping over the puddles.

After she had eaten, Madge was in the bathroom for ages. Mother couldn't understand it.

"You'll get waterlogged, my girl," she called.

Madge turned the taps full on to drown the sound of her cough. Alan thought she might put on a dress and her Sunday coat, but she came down in her old skirt and blouse.

"You're not to go," he said firmly, looking anxiously at her pale face.

"I must," she whispered. "I promised." She jammed the frayed panama on to her head and began to fasten the buttons of her raincoat. Mother shouted from the kitchen for them to get out of the hall and stop making a mess.

"You're being a fool," he said. "Can't you see how reckless you're being?"

"It'll happen some time," she said reasonably.

"It happens to everybody sooner or later. If it's got to be this soon, I'd rather it was someone I know."

She was watching him intently as though she hoped he would still say something to prevent her going. Something vital and conclusive. He couldn't think of anything.

As she opened the door it stopped raining.

"You see," she said miserably. "It's a sign. It's meant to be."

He took hold of her arm.

"If you go out into that garden, I'll tell on you. I will."

"Silly old Alan," she said. "You know you won't. What difference would it make? I can run faster than them. They'd have to nail me to the fence."

She walked backwards down the path, taking her time, waiting for him to come up with a convincing argument. Her face looked desperate, like the time she'd been sent to the chiropodist to have a corn removed. She'd wanted him to prevent that too.

After a moment she disappeared behind next door's hedge. When he ran on to the pavement, expecting to see her huddled against the lampost, he was outraged to observe her sprinting along the road, head back and arms moving like pistons, in the direction of the railway crossing.

Mother went upstairs to lie down. He hovered on the landing, trying to think how he could tell her about Madge. She called out fiercely: "Get away you big lout. Can't you find something to do?"

200

He trailed downstairs and went into the garden. The sky had cleared, the grass glittered under the weak sunlight. Father had emerged from the greenhouse and was staring gloomily at his flooded vegetable patch.

"Blasted climate," he said. "Nothing but a quagmire."

"Madge has gone out again," said Alan.

"If I had my way," said Father. "I'd pack the whole thing in and sell it back to the council. Let them breed crocodiles in it." He squelched toward the fence, calling over his shoulder: "I suppose your mother's gone out too. They're a pair, they are." And he gave a short hoot of laughter that was borne away on the wind.

"She's not gone anywhere," he said. "She never does."

"Ahh!" said Father, full of contempt.

"She's got nowhere to go. She sits down at the station every night, on her own in the waiting room."

Father turned and looked at him. "Fine tale," he sneered. "Do you think I'm soft in the head?" He brought up his boot, clogged with mud, to stamp the spade into the earth.

"She can't stand being in the same room with you," cried Alan. His whole body started to tremble. "You make her sick. You make her flesh creep."

Father stood there leaning on his spade. Gradually his head began to wobble as if someone was shaking him by the throat. Watching him, Alan was consumed with malice. He felt light and powerful as though a weight had shifted from him. He turned and ran back up the lawn, muttering, as he leapt in one bound over the privet hedge, "You mean old bastard, you bastard, you rotten old bastard." He kicked open the scullery door, not caring if he disturbed Mother, and stood in the kitchen with his arms stretched above his head, both fists tightly clenched. It couldn't last. After a few moments he didn't feel vindictive any more, only worn out. He slumped guiltily at the table, not daring to look out of the back window in case Father lay face downwards in the mud beneath the poplar trees. For a while he was frightened at what he had done but then he remembered all the times his father had said things to hurt Mother and Madge and himself. He'd forgotten most of them; they were only words spat out in anger. He was encouraged by the sound of Father running busily up and down the path; his beret bobbed past the window. Presently, from the porch, came the sound of wood being sawn.

Father wasn't prostrate with grief. He was cutting another square of board to replace the shattered glass—something to keep out the rain until the glazier came.

"Alan," called Mother.

He didn't answer at once. She was always shouting orders for refreshment, as if she lived over a tea shop.

"Alan," she cried again, urgently.

He went into the hall.

"He's cutting down the tree," she said,

crouched at the top of the stairs in her underskirt.

Father stood on the rockery with his back to the porch, one hand braced against the thin trunk of the sycamore. The saw, old and rusty as it was, had bitten deep into the wood.

"It'll fall the wrong way," screamed Mother appearing at the upstairs window. "He'll bring down the fence."

He ran on to the grass, to the far side of the rockery.

"Stop it," he shouted. "Stop it."

Even as he spoke the saw buckled in Father's hand, snagged on a knot within the trunk. Father gave a little gasp and let go of the handle. He leaned against the tree and slithered slowly downwards to sit on the whitewashed stones. His eyes were shut.

"Joe?" said Alan.

He bent forward and touched his father's jaw stained green from the wood.

Father opened his eyes. "Help me in, son."

There was something different about his face, something fixed, as if the skin had frozen to the bone. He leaned heavily on Alan but there was no substance to him.

"Take his boots off," cried Mother, barring the way up the stairs. "You'll ruin my carpet."

Father gave a little snigger.

"Ring the doctor," ordered Alan.

"Don't talk soft," said Mother.

"Damn you to hell," he shouted. "Look at his face."

Mother couldn't see Father's face because he was half turned, nestling like a child with his cheek against Alan's shoulder. All the same she let him pass. She watched them climb the stairs before going into the front room.

He laid his father on the bed and tugged off his boots. He didn't want to disturb him too much, so he went and fetched blankets from the settle and covered him over, right up to the chin.

"It tickles," said Father peevishly, clawing at the covers.

Alan would have liked to hide his father's face, the high arch of his waxen nose, the dull eyes, grey as pebbles, restlessly gazing at the walls. He could hear Mother's voice, excited and important, talking on the telephone. She laughed shrilly, several times.

"What's she on about?" said Father. "Doesn't she realize I'm a sick man?"

"Hush," Alan said. "It's only her way."

He walked up and down the room wondering how long the doctor would take. He might be out playing golf. Why didn't his mother come up? He thought he heard someone crying in the kitchen below.

"Shall I get the brandy?" he asked.

"Do that," said Father. His voice seemed to come from some distance. He lay perfectly still.

Madge was in the kitchen, hunched in a chair, crying with her hands over her face. Mother was at the mirror combing her hair, titivating for the doctor.

"Hush up," he said to Madge. "It's nothing much. You mustn't worry."

"Is he still in his dirty old clothes?" asked Mother. "Did you think to change the pillow slips?"

"I changed nothing," he shouted.

He walked out of the back door and along the garden without knowing what he was doing. He watched his feet sinking into the damp grass with every step he took. There was one solitary daffodil beginning to open in the stony border beside the fence. He went into the house and told Mother to take the brandy upstairs.

"What a fuss about nothing," she said. "Heaven knows what the doctor will think, called out on a Saturday afternoon."

Madge cried louder than ever.

"Be quiet," he told her. "You won't help Father making a noise like that."

She took her hands from her face and he saw her swollen eyelids and her nose all gummy with mucous.

"He's gone," she sobbed. "He went early this morning. I never saw him."

"Is that the doctor?" he said, thinking he heard a car.

"I'll never see him again. Never in all my life."

"You shut up," he cried fiercely. "There's nothing wrong with him. He just needs a bit of rest."

"Alan," cried Mother. "He's here."

He ran into the hall and let the doctor in.

Mother came down smiling and held out her hand.

"Good afternoon," she said graciously. "So sorry to disturb you like this."

Alan pushed past her and went up the stairs to look at Father. He had more color in his face now. Please, he thought, let him be ill a little while longer . . . just till the doctor's seen him.

They were coming upstairs. Father struggled upright in the bed and looked sheepishly toward the door.

"What a dreary day it is," said the doctor, walking to the window and gazing into the garden. "Rain . . . always rain."

He reached down and held Father's wrist. Mother went away to see to Madge.

"I do beg your pardon," remarked Father civilly. "I think I'm going to faint." And he lay back on the pillow and closed his eyes.

The doctor stood a second, feeling his pulse. Then he let go of his hand and pulled roughly at the blankets. He seized Father by the front of his battledress and hauled him half off the bed.

"Help me," he shouted to Alan. "Get him on the floor."

They bundled Father on to the cold lino. His hat fell off. The doctor straddled his stomach and punched him in the chest. Over and over. One potato, two potato, three potato, four—

It seemed to Alan, crouched there on his knees holding Father's hand, thumb tipped with sticking plaster, that the doctor was knocking at a door, demanding to be admitted. Only there was nobody in.

One of the first things Mother did, after they had taken the body away in an ambulance, was to chuck the A.R.P. hat into the dustbin.

H E WAITED a moment at the top of the station hill still holding the flowers Madge had given him, looking down at the rows of houses that stretched clear to the distant pines. He thought Joan might have come to meet him. She had a part-time job in Southport and most days she had the use of the car.

He went briskly down the steps to the road, averting his eyes from the old perambulators and rusted stoves that hooligans had flung over the railings on to the once grassy slopes where the crocuses had bloomed. He walked slowly, noting the decaying bungalows behind the privet hedges. His own house was spick and span, freshly painted every five years. He knew a man in town who let him have the paint at cost price.

He turned the corner and crossed the road. It

209

was a pity about the council estate, but then he supposed people had to live somewhere. The houses were quite decent; there were ornaments in the windows. Fancy Madge wanting the dancing lady. It was only made of plaster. It was just as well Madge hadn't asked to come and stay for a few days. There wasn't that much room.

Approaching the house, he hesitated. He wondered if Joan had one of her headaches. Now that the children were older and more independent, he feared she was sometimes lonely. She spent a lot of time sitting upstairs pretending to do her football pools. It wasn't her fault. She'd had an unhappy childhood. She didn't come from a close family, not like him and Madge.

Turning his back on the house, in case his wife watched from the window, he let the flowers spill from his folded newspaper on to the pavement. Then, squaring his shoulders, he walked up the path.